JINGLEBELL JANE

MAIL ORDER BRIDES RESCUE SERIES, BOOK #7

JO GRAFFORD, WRITING AS
JOVIE GRACE

ISBN: 978-1-63907-021-3

GET A FREE BOOK!

Join my mailing list to be the first to know about new releases, free books, special discount prices, Bonus Content, and giveaways.

https://BookHip.com/GNVABPD

ACKNOWLEDGMENTS

Many thanks to my beta readers and editor, Cathleen Weaver, for working their magic on this story. I am also wildly grateful to my Cuppa Jo Readers on Facebook for reading and loving my books!

ABOUT THIS SERIES

The only mail order bride company with an insurance policy enforced by the Gallant Rescue Society — *No extra cost!*

The Gallant Rescue Society Oath

"I hereby solemnly pledge my gun and my honor to the Gallant Rescue Society.

To be called upon day or night.

To rescue any Bride-To-Be from any undesirable circumstance on her journey to meet her Groom.

To return her (if at all possible) with her virtue intact to the Boomtown Mail Order Brides Company.

No questions asked.

So help me, God."

CHAPTER 1: CAPTURED

JANE

*I*t was the first week of November, normally Jane Sherrington's favorite time of year. She idly traced a finger down one of the iron bars of her jail cell. What few trees, shrubs, and flowers there were in the deserts of Arizona would be shedding their leaves and blooms by now. The air would be getting brisk at night — more than likely a degree or two cooler than when she'd been captured a week earlier. Eight days, three hours, and twenty-one minutes to be precise.

She was very accurate at keeping time. If asked, she could recite to the minute how long it had been since she and her brother, Hunter, had run away from the home of their horrid uncle, who'd proven to be an equally horrid guardian. She could recount how many years, months, and weeks they had been on the road and how many trains and stagecoaches he and his comrades had held up at gunpoint and robbed. She also knew exactly how many days her brother had been missing from their camp, high on the Rose de la Montaña, which was the only reason he'd avoided capture like herself and the rest of his gang. What she didn't know was when he would return for her. All she knew was that he would.

And the thought terrified her.

"Miss Sherrington, let us try this again, shall we?" Sheriff Chase Otera had a sigh in his voice and a sympathetic glint in his dark gaze, as he pulled up a chair outside her cell. He took a seat and pulled out his list of handwritten questions she'd refused to answer thus far.

He was roughly the age her father would have been if he was still alive, and she could tell it troubled him greatly to have a woman housed in his jail. His sympathies had worked to her advantage, though. So far, his kindness had garnered her a pillow and a soft wool blanket, a fresh change of clothing, and a tiny sliver of apple pie. Alas, it had garnered her nothing in which to pick a lock or otherwise escape her confinement.

"To the best of your knowledge, Miss Sherrington, where is your brother?"

She remained standing in front of the bars separating them, but she lowered her lashes. It didn't matter how many questions he asked, her answer was the same.

I do not know.

With a grimace at her silence, he moved on to his next question. "Do you know what heist he is planning next?"

I do not know.

She wished she knew. Quite honestly, she couldn't state with any clarity if her brother was even still alive. It had always been like this between them. He came and went as he pleased, often being gone days or weeks at a time. Because of the number of lawmen who had him on their most wanted lists, she never knew when his next visit would be or if it would be his last. Such were the risks of living a life of crime.

Jane tried not to wince with each question as the sheriff of Headstone worked his way through his long list, bracing herself for the hardest one — the one with which he always ended his interrogations. She blinked back tears, because it was a topic that haunted her day and night. Forcing her eyes wide open in the attempt to control her emotions, she blindly fastened her gaze on the shiny silver badge fastened to the breast pocket of his vest. She respected what it stood for and longed more than anything to be on the other side of these iron bars...on the right side of the law. Her heart was already there. It had always been there.

"Will your brother come back for you, Miss Sherrington?"

"I do not know!" The answer wrenched itself from her before she could call it back, stunning them both with the fact she'd broken her silence at last. It was a relief to finally bear her soul to the kindhearted sheriff; however, terror clenched her insides. Terror at what her brother might do if he found out she had cooperated with the investigation. Nobody ratted anybody out in their gang. It was their number one rule in the event of capture. Nobody talked. *Ever!*

"I, er...thank you for answering the question." The sheriff shifted in his seat, fiddled with his pen and paper, and appeared to be struggling to overcome his amazement. "I know this whole ordeal has been difficult for you, ma'am."

"It is," she said in a voice barely above a whisper.

"But if you will simply finish answering my questions, there is a distinct possibility I may be able to let you go free."

Free. The word made her tears spring forth in a full gush. She wanted her freedom more than anything in the world, but she would never be free — not while Hunter Sherrington was on the loose.

"I do not know," she repeated in a shaky voice. "It is my only answer to every one of your questions, sir. I am telling the truth. I quite simply do not know. I never do. My brother keeps his own council."

He confided in no one, not even to MaryAnne Branson, whom he'd most unwittingly made his second-in-charge. MaryAnne, as it turned out, had been turned by a group of federal marshals during a previous capture and had returned to the gang in an undercover role for the sole purpose of assisting in their arrest. Which she had done in spades. Everyone in Hunter Sherrington's gang was now behind bars, including his own sister — everyone, that is, except Hunter Sherrington, himself.

"Miss Branson said the same. Your story agrees with hers one hundred percent." Sheriff Otera stood and scrubbed a hand wearily across his jaw. It was getting late, and an evening shadow was manifesting itself across the lower half of his face. "In fact, every member of your brother's gang, whom we have in our custody, shares the same story about your involvement. Though none can offer any proof, every one of them claims you are innocent of all wrongdoing. Is that also true, Miss Sherrington?"

Am I innocent? Jane made no effort to dash away the tears still trickling one over the other down her cheeks. She didn't feel innocent. She felt older than her years. Bitter. Jaded. "I know what sort of man my brother is, sheriff. I think I've always known." She understood the circumstances leading up to his decision to step outside the boundaries of the law, but she also understood that he was wrong — very wrong. She'd spent the last five of her seventeen years trying to change his mind, trying to coax him into leaving his criminal activities behind.

She averted her face from the sheriff, no longer able to bear the concern and sympathy mirrored in his fatherly gaze. She was the sister of a notorious criminal. Nothing would ever remove the stain from her name or reputation, and that was that. She could drift and she could survive, but she would never belong anywhere.

The sound of metal clanging against metal made her jump. "What are you doing, sir?" she gasped, whipping her face around. Unless she was dreaming or imagining things, he was unlocking her jail cell.

"Letting you go," he returned mildly. "You answered my questions, and I am a man of my word."

"But—" She raised and lowered her hands. *I have no place to go. No money. No friends.* At one point, she'd considered MaryAnne Branson to be her friend, but she was no longer so sure. The woman hadn't hesitated to rat out the entire gang and land them in jail. Not to mention, she'd made a dangerous enemy of Hunter in the process.

He would exact his revenge on her, in his own way and in his own time. It would be swift and thorough. Jane would just as soon not be caught in the crossfire when that day came.

"I imagine it will take a little time to get back on your feet, so to speak." Sheriff Otera opened her cell door wide and eyed her in concern. "Since it's getting late, I've arranged for a lovely townswoman by the name of Felicity Barra to board you for the night. She's an attorney, in the event you wish to seek legal council."

A woman who is an attorney? Jane stared at him in awe.

"Her husband, Levi, runs a ranch across town, has three younger brothers, and all of them are part-owners in the yellow diamond mine over yonder at Hope's Landing."

Diamonds? A shiver of foreboding worked its way through Jane's slender shoulders. As soon as her brother caught wind of it, another heist would be in the making. "That is very kind of you," she mumbled. "I do not know how I will ever be able to repay you." More than likely, her only "payment" would come in the form of a rabid brother who would tear his way through Headstone, exacting revenge for the capture of his sister and comrades.

"Think nothing of it." He waved a hand in dismissal. "It's the least we can do to recompense you for the length of your detainment. I'll send a deputy to fetch my wagon, and I'll drive you there myself."

As the sheriff's wagon rolled down Main Street, Jane fingered the long blonde braid trailing over her shoulder, wondering what Felicity and Levi Barra would be like. Would they be kind? Suspicious of her? Vengeful in attitude after all the horrible things the Sherrington gang had done?

They drove past the town square, and she caught her breath at the sight of the Christmas tree on display. Red ribbons draped it, and candles flickered from the outermost branches. At the very top, a metal star caught the fading sunlight and glowed a rosy gold.

"We had the tree lighting last night," Sheriff Otera offered. "Wish you could have attended it." He sounded regretful.

She stared at him in wonder. What kind of sheriff cared about frivolous stuff like that? Didn't he have his hands full processing all the indictments of the Sherrington gang members?

"Ah, here we are." He nosed his team of horses up a long, hard-packed earthen drive. A wide, sprawling farmhouse rose in the distance. It looked freshly whitewashed and boasted a wide, inviting front veranda. A dog barked, cows mooed, and the dying shoots of what used to be a cornfield waved dryly in the evening breezes.

A tall, slim cowboy was lounged against one of the posts at the top of the porch stairs. He pushed away from his post and straightened at their approach.

"Well, what do you know? That looks like Dodge." Sheriff Otera slowed his horses and brought them to a standstill in front of the farmhouse. "He's the youngest Barra brother, the only one that isn't married yet. He's but seventeen, maybe eighteen. Think I recall hearing something about a birthday not too long ago."

Just like me. I am seventeen. She squinted through the twilight, trying to get a better look at the lad. She couldn't remember the last time she'd encountered someone her age. Sure, she saw them in passing in the towns her brother and his cronies were about to rob, but she'd never been allowed to engage them in any way. To learn their names. Or hold a conversation.

She swayed in her seat, feeling suddenly off balance. What would she say to him, when she had the chance? How should she act? They might as well have been raised on different planets for how little they would have in common. More than likely, this Dodge Barra had grown up with a roof over his head and three square meals a day, not to mention a proper education. She'd had none of those things.

He loped down the stairs two at a time and swaggered to her side of the carriage.

She stared at him with a mixture of fear and fascination and discovered no censure in his dark eyes, only curiosity and shrewd speculation.

He was dressed humbly in faded denim trousers, scuffed boots, and a plaid shirt rolled at the sleeves. She was surprised at how tanned and muscular his arms were.

Doffing a well-worn brown Stetson, he revealed longish blue-black locks that tangled roguishly with his collar. He certainly didn't look like the owner of a diamond mine.

"Howdy there, sheriff." He shot a devilish grin across the wagon seat to her escort. "I gather this young lady is the

Jinglebell Jane everyone across town has been carrying on about?"

Jinglebell Jane. She caught her breath, feeling her heartbeat race in excitement. No one had ever teased her like that, nor had she ever before possessed a nickname. It was so fun and unexpected...so freakishly normal!

CHAPTER 2: SUSPICIONS

DODGE

*D*odge studied the play of emotions across Jane's features and was shocked to note a mix of surprise, wistfulness, and cautious pleasure. If he didn't know better, he'd assume she actually liked his nickname for her; but he did know better. Jane Sherrington was the sister of one of the most notorious criminals in the west. Her heart was stained with crime. Whether by her own hands or by direct association, it hardly mattered. There was not an innocent bone in her body, and he'd be wise to remember it.

"Oh, there you are!" His sister-in-law, Felicity Barra, breezed out the front door and flew down the porch stairs to join their huddle beside the wagon. Her chestnut hair was twisted up in a complex set of twists and swirls like only a woman can do, and her green velvet skirts billowed around her ankles. She was dressed fancy, because his oldest brother, Levi, had decided to escort his bride to the theater this evening. "You must be Jane Sherrington." She held out both hands to Jane.

Looking even more surprised by Felicity's kind reception than his own playful greeting, Jane was slow to reach back.

When she finally grasped Felicity's hands, she seemed to be blinking away mist in her eyes. "I am most grateful for your invitation to stay the night," her voice held a slight tremor, "seeing as I truly had no other place else to go."

"Bah!" Felicity tossed her head as if to make light of the girl's tremulous claim. "It's way too soon to decide how long you'll be staying. I've fluffed up the pillows on the bed in our guest room and shoved the dust around a little to hide it as best I could." She winked to acknowledge her jest. "How about we just get you settled in and take it one day at a time?"

"May we? Really?" Jane blinked rapidly several times. "I, er, I thank you from the bottom of my heart, Mrs. Barra." She swallowed hard and managed to look a trifle faint.

Oh, she knew how to put on a good act! Dodge folded his arms and tried to muffle a chuckle, which somehow came out as a snort.

The heads of both women swiveled in his direction. Jane looked mortified, and a pink flush tinged her cheeks, whereas Felicity looked surprised at first and then mildly admonishing. She gave Dodge a slight shake of her head as if *he'd* been the one to do something wrong, all the while *she* was the one who'd opened the door of their home to a known criminal. Or criminal by association...

Blast it all! Dodge was having a difficult time keeping the details straight. One thing was clear, however. With the way Felicity was fawning all over Jane and the way Levi always fawned all over Felicity, it was going to be up to Dodge to sort through the mess slowly curling its way through their midst; and he had the perfect plan in mind.

If his sister-in-law wanted him to cool his heels and cozy up to their attractive little houseguest despite her sullied reputation, fine! He could be as congenial as a pig slopping through his favorite pit of waller, but that didn't mean he couldn't do a little personal investigating on the side all private-like. Come to think of it, he might even choke down his elephant-sized reservations and pretend to befriend the little filly. That would keep his sister-in-law happy *and* allow him to get close enough to Jane to do some real digging into her sordid life.

His mind made up, Dodge unwound his arms and forced a welcoming smile to his face. Who cared if it felt like his cheeks might crack from the effort? Hunter Sherrington was a dangerous criminal to have on the loose around this part of the country, and Dodge's gut told him Hunter's sister would be the key to bringing him down. With a little luck, he might be able to bring down both siblings at the same time. Dodge had no doubt whatsoever he was going to discover Jane wasn't nearly as innocent as she appeared. There was just no way in tarnation. She could bat her pretty eyelashes at everyone else, but he wasn't falling for her games. According to the other criminals Sheriff Otera had in custody, Jane had been embedded with their gang for years. Not days, but more than three years!

"Welcome to the Barra ranch," he declared a might stiffly, holding out one large, callused hand. "I'm Dodge, and I reckon we can find something for you to do around here. Plenty of chickens to feed, cows to milk, and horses to brush down." Unlike Levi and his second oldest brother, Tennyson, who lately had taken to dressing and acting like polished gentlemen, Dodge never bothered wearing gloves around the ranch or pretending to be anything other than what he was — a dusty, scarred cowboy. Even Prescott, his other brother who was but a mere two years his senior, had taken to acting all debonair since he married Daisy. Dodge missed his brothers' carefree days before the first three of them had gotten themselves hitched to brides. He missed their bull riding, card playing, devil-may-care existence when their finances were a little less certain but their lives were more interesting.

"I don't rightly know about that, Dodge," Felicity cut in softly. "Jane's just arrived. There's no rush to toss her out in the barnyard just yet."

To Dodge's extreme interest, however, Jane didn't bat an eye at his suggestion that she might be put to work around the ranch instead of living there for free. "I'd like that very much," she confessed in a shy voice, clasping his hand. "I don't want to impose. If I can be of any help at all..." She let her offer rest in an open-handed manner.

He was unprepared for the fierce, full handshake she gave him and the bold way she stared right into his eyes, all man-to-man like. It was unsettling, to say the least, and in direct contrast to the shy tone of her voice. As he suspected, she had plenty of backbone in her and then some. The shy voice was probably just part of her act.

"It's been a long time since I tossed a bucket of cracked corn to a flock of hens," she continued in a stronger voice, "but I've never milked a cow. Not once. I reckon you're more than up to the task of showing me how, Mr. Barra." Her blonde brows arched, and her blue eyes glinted a challenge. Then her gaze dropped to their hands, which, for reasons Dodge couldn't explain, were still joined.

Ah! His fault. He could feel the heat of a flush creeping up the sides of his neck. He had no idea why he was still gripping her hand. Inwardly shaking his head, he let it go. "You can drop the mister. There are plenty enough Mr. Barras running around Headstone these days. It's just Dodge, and I can show you how to milk a cow if you're really all that interested." He tried to sound offhand, as if it didn't matter to him.

Sheriff Otera hopped back into the driver's seat of his rig and tipped his hat at them. "Well, I've done my part. Looks like this new arrangement is working out just fine. I'm thinking now would be a good time for me to mosey back to the station before Dodge puts *me* to work in the barnyard out yonder."

Felicity chuckled, and Jane waved as he drove away.

The first thing Dodge noted after the sheriff's wagon disappeared on the horizon was that Jane didn't have anything but the clothes on her back. No travel bag. No reticule. Just a plain and rather manly looking brown dress. It was threadbare at the elbows, and there was a rip at the seam near the toes of her scuffed black boots.

Catching his eye, Jane raised her chin. From her heightened color, he perceived she was either angry at his perusal or embarrassed at the sorry state of her clothing, but he couldn't be sure which was the case.

Felicity lightly touched a hand to Jane's shoulder as she urged her towards the porch stairs. "We're about the same height and build, don't you think?" she asked companionably. "I've a lovely blue velvet gown that just came back from a mending at the dressmaker's. I tripped my way up these very stairs the other day and ripped the hem. So if you don't mind wearing a castoff that's undergone a few much-needed repairs, my dear, I think it will do nicely for our family dinner this evening."

Jane made a curious little gasping sound and nodded her head furiously, though she didn't say anything. Dodge was walking behind the two women, so he couldn't see Jane's face.

Once inside the foyer, he tried to duck around Jane to get a better look at her. However, her head was bent as Felicity herded her straight for the stairwell leading to the second level.

"Let's draw you a bath, my dear, shall we? There's a fire going in the guest room, so you won't freeze to a complete icicle."

Jane made another half-muffled, snuffling sound and

stumbled on the first rung of the stairs, as if failing to see it. Her mussed blonde braid slid around her shoulder to dangle down the front of her dress.

Without thinking, Dodge lunged across the foyer, boots clomping on the plank flooring, to grasp her elbow.

"I th-thank you," she muttered damply, without looking up.

This time, Dodge was close enough to determine why her voice sounded so strange. Fat globs of tears were running down her dusty cheeks, leaving muddy trails.

What in tarnation? He hastily dropped his hand and stepped back to give her some privacy.

Felicity shot him a warning look over her shoulder and shook her head, as if urging him not to say anything more.

He nodded, crossing his arms and frowning at the backs of the two women as they made their way up the stairs. He knew Jane Sherrington was a fraud, so her tears had to be part of her act; but, blast it all! The salt drops on her face sure looked genuine. He was going to have to really watch his step around her. The chit was far more clever than he'd first given her credit for. Why, Felicity was fast falling beneath her charms, and he'd be next if he wasn't careful!

Dodge slowly backed away from the stairs, pivoted right a few degrees, and headed on through the foyer. He marched down the hall leading to the rear of the house. Tennyson had been the first brother to marry and leave home. Their half-sister, Madge, had moved out next, shortly before Levi married Felicity. Then, Prescott had moved out to marry Meg, leaving Dodge as the last unmarried brother living at home. Dodge had quickly moved his few sparse belongings to the old servant's quarters Madge had vacated beside the kitchen to give Levi and Felicity as much privacy as possible.

Even so, Dodge couldn't wait until the day he could move out and live on his own. Levi was busy having his attorney wife help him deed off various parcels of property as gifts to each brother when they got married. Since Dodge was the youngest at seventeen — almost eighteen — Levi had saved his deed for last, telling Dodge he could remain living at home for as long as he wished. Though Dodge knew Levi meant well, Dodge didn't require a nursemaid. Maybe some lads his age needed the oversight, but he wasn't one of those creatures. A lifetime of hardships had forced all four Barra brothers to grow up quickly, else they'd have never survived.

Their mother had passed before her time, and their father had all but abandoned them the next several years while he grieved and wallowed in his memories. Initially, they'd claim jumped the ranch, but eventually (and with Felicity's help), they'd come to own the deed free and clear. Through a series of rather bizarre and extraordinary events, they'd also become part owners of the yellow diamond mine on the edge of town, called Hope's Landing.

That was where Dodge spent most of his days, not working on the ranch like he'd led Jane to believe. They had a hired staff for that, leaving him free to put the horses through their paces in the afternoons following his duties at the mine. However, Jingebell Jane didn't need to know that just yet. Dodge couldn't wait to sit her conniving self on a wooden stool in the barn and watch her muddle her way through her first milking.

Instead of heading to his room, Dodge ducked inside the kitchen. Call it a curse, but he nearly always felt half-starved — all hours of the day and night. Maybe it was because he'd spent too many of his teen years fighting hunger pains while trying to help his brothers eke out a living. Things were much better now with the yellow diamond mine income padding their existence, but Dodge had yet to forget the hunger pains.

Felicity joined him before he finished raiding the leftovers from breakfast. "We need to talk, Dodge." She looked so distressed that he slowly lowered the piece of bacon he was in the process of raising to his mouth.

"Are you well?" he asked, shooting to his feet so quickly that he nearly knocked over his stool. "Did that scamp harm you in any way?" He righted the stool and scooted it back under the cabinet.

"What?" She looked astounded and raised a finger to point to the guest room upstairs, which happened to be located directly over their heads. "You mean Jane?"

He gave a grim nod.

"No! Of course not!" she cried, then lowered her voice with a guilty look. "How could you say such a thing? Why, the poor mite is barely—"

"The closest kin to a notorious criminal," he finished for her, slapping his hands down on the wooden cabinet top between them. "I know she's putting on a good act for everyone, but you can't possibly be fooled. You're an attorney, for crying out loud!"

Felicity straightened her shoulders. "I am, indeed." Her voice was cool. "I don't suppose you think she was acting out all the scars I just witnessed riddling her back and shoulder blades." She moved around him with a swish of skirts to remove three mugs from a shelf. She proceeded to fill them from the tea kettle on the stove. Steam swirled enticingly over the top of each mug.

His gaze narrowed in suspicion. "Scars?" he asked carefully. "What sort of scars?"

She shot him a look full of righteous indignation. "Not recent ones. That I can tell you. As for how she acquired them, well, I reckon that will take winning her confidence first. Alas, trust won't come easy to a girl like her. She's as jumpy as a wild filly. That's where you come in."

"Me! How?" He wasn't certain he liked where the conversation was heading. He also very much didn't like the thought of anyone harming a young woman, not even one who might be a criminal.

"You're about her age. She'll be able to relate to you better than anyone else if you give her half a chance," she trained a motherly scolding eye on him, "which you haven't so far."

"I—"

"All you've done is stare and frown and taunt her. She's going to need more than that, Dodge, if we're going to make this work." She spread her hands to take in their home and furnishings. "She's going to need a friend."

He shook his head and glanced away from his sister-in-law's shrewd, pointed gaze. Trust went in two directions. He had no reason to trust Jane and had every intention of seeing her back behind bars soon.

"And a tutor," Felicity continued in a firm voice.

He scowled. "What do you mean? She should have already graduated or be close to it." He'd graduated last year, himself.

"Should be." His sister-in-law nodded. "On that, we can agree; but the fact remains, our lovely guest cannot read or write. Heaven only knows what kind of childhood she had to endure. My gut tells me there is much we don't know about her yet. Therefore, I am going to recommend to Levi that we enroll her in school right away."

His eyebrows shot to the ceiling. "You mean, you expect her to live with us...indefinitely?" *Good gravy!* This he'd not been expecting.

"She has no where else to go," Felicity reminded. "She swallowed her pride long enough to admit that to us."

Or so Jane wants us to believe! It wasn't like Felicity to be so naive.

"And no money, I suspect."

That we know of... The chit had been living with a den of

robbers. No doubt she had a cache somewhere. Dodge mentally added it to his list of things to investigate.

"Without any formal training, she cannot hope to find much in the way of a job." Felicity sighed and drummed her fingers on the cabinet. "So if we're going to do the right thing by this young woman, she'll be attending school." She stopped her tapping and glanced up at Dodge with pleading in her eyes. "With the amount of time I have to spend at the legal office downtown, I'm going to be depending on you to help her with her homework."

Dodge snorted. He couldn't believe his ears. Jane really had pulled the wool over his sister-in-law's eyes. More's the pity. Looked like it was going to be up to him — entirely up to him — to uncover the wench's true colors for all to see. It shouldn't be too hard when Hunter Sherrington showed up in the flesh, and his sister willingly joined forces with him once again.

"Have it your way, madam sister-in-law." He winked at Felicity. She was accustomed to his teasing and would find his current subterfuge more believable if he continued to heckle her a bit. "I might could help our guest a bit with her letters, numbers, and such."

"Might could?" She raised her silky dark brows at him. "You do realize I want her to learn *proper* spelling and grammar, not Dodge Barra's barnyard dialect?"

"Yes'm." He inclined his head in false submission. "Can't rightly expect her to land a highfalutin job like yours, iffen she don't get some good learnin' under her belt."

Felicity stared at him for a moment before she burst out laughing. "Oh, Dodge! For a moment there, you truly had me worried." She shook her head, still chuckling. "What are we going to do with you?"

He grinned at her. "I'm a fella. All you need to do is keep feeding me."

Her smile remained, but her gaze grew calculating. "That I can do. How does dinner at six o'clock sound to you?"

"Like a dream come true." He swiped another two slices of bacon from the platter on the cabinet before heading for the back door.

"Good. You can show your appreciation for my pot roast by giving Jane her first tutoring session after dinner."

His steps slowed. *Surely you jest.*

"I borrowed a few textbooks and a slate from Callie this morning." Callie was Tennyson's wife and the schoolmarm out at Hope's Landing.

I reckon that means you're not jesting. With a groan of surrender, Dodge pushed open the door and stepped outside where he could breathe again.

CHAPTER 3: OLD AND NEW WOUNDS

JANE

*J*ane stood in front of a long antique oval mirror in the Barra's guest chamber and stared. As promised, Felicity had lent her a blue velvet dress. Real velvet! She ran her hands wonderingly down the bodice and full skirts. *Unbelievable!*

Jane hardly recognized herself. After more than three years on the road wearing whatever items of ill-fitting clothing she could scrounge up, this was like stepping into a fairytale. *Maybe it's all just one big wonderful dream. That's it. I must be dreaming.* Jane gave her arm a none too gentle pinch through the fabric.

"Ouch!" *Very well. I am not dreaming.* She blinked at herself in the mirror. Her damp blonde hair should have been her first clue that she was wide awake. What a luxury it had been to take an honest-to-heavens bath for the first time in…she couldn't remember how long it had been. Jane gazed around the room, feeling suddenly dizzy. Since she was truly awake, it meant the velvet dress was real, the four-poster bed in the center of the room was real, the patchwork quilt tucked around the mattress was real…

Oh, my! She took a stumbling few steps and plopped down on a wide, weathered trunk at the base of the bed. There was a stacked stone hearth directly across from her, a small roughly hewn writing table and chair to her left, and a simple but serviceable white porcelain basin to her right. It was a lovely room, and it was entirely hers to use for now. The mistress of the house had made it quite clear that Jane was free to stay as long as she liked.

Until Hunter came to whisk her away…

Jane closed her eyes against a rush of longing to see him again and know that he was safe and well. However, her longing was mixed with dread at the thought of leaving Headstone. In her short stay there, she'd grown rather attached to a few things. Things most folks probably took for granted — like a roof over her head and regular meals. Oh, and a few other small items like not having to dodge bullets and arrest all the time.

The clock on the mantle chimed out the hour, making her jolt. It was five o'clock already. According to Felicity, Jane would be expected to appear at the dinner table downstairs at six. She gave a muffled snort of laughter. *Dinner at a table.* Mercy! Gathering around a table was something most folks probably took for granted. For her, however, it was going to be a rare treat.

She pushed to her feet and moved closer to the fire to speed up her hair drying. A swift glance around the room helped her locate a brush and a handful of hairpins resting on the cabinet next to the wash basin. She retrieved the brush and returned to the fire, drawing it slowly through her waist-length locks. By a quarter 'til six, it was dry enough for her to twist up in a thick knot behind her head. It was a plain hair style, but it was the best she could do on such short notice. Her time on the road hadn't exactly called for primping, so she was sorely out of practice. After a scowl of irritation at herself in the mirror, she reached up and tugged a few strands from her bun to dangle past her temple and cheeks. There. It wasn't fancy, but at least it was less severe looking.

Her scuffed black boots would have to do, but the dress would be long enough to hide them when she reached the bottom of the stairs. With one last anxious look around her, Jane left the safety of her bedchamber and headed down the stairs.

Dodge Barra banged open the front door and stomped inside just as she reached the bottom of the stairs. Looking surprised to see her standing on the last rung, he swept off his black Stetson and treated her to a mock bow. "After you, Jinglebell Jane." He ushered her inside the dining room to her right, his left.

She was equally surprised at the sight of him. For one thing, he'd changed for dinner. Instead of the dusty riding gear he'd worn earlier, he was now sporting a black suit and a white dress shirt with a black and silver bolo at his throat.

"Thank you, Mister er, Dodge." She hated the heat she felt rising to her cheeks and wished she could just relax and act normally around the swaggering cowboy. It didn't help that he was devilishly handsome with his longish blue-black hair scraping his shirt collar, darkly tanned features, and scarred and callused hands that were a little at odds with the slicked-up rest of him.

"Just Dodge," he reminded shortly.

Right. She resisted the urge to roll her eyes at his prickliness. Unlike the warm and welcoming Felicity Barra, Dodge beheld her with no small amount of suspicion in his dark gaze. She wasn't certain why it bothered her, since it was more what she'd been expecting from the town folks, more what she deserved.

Dodge followed her into the dining room, where she stopped so short that he bumped into her from behind.

"My pardon," he muttered in a low voice that didn't sound overly apologetic. He briefly clutched the underside of her elbow, as if to ensure her footing, a gesture she found oddly gallant despite his obvious disapproval of her.

It was enough to give her the courage to face the giant standing at the head of the table. *Mercy!* Jane resisted the urge to press a hand to her rapidly pounding heart. She'd never encountered such a large creature in her life. He dwarfed most of the men in her brother's gang, and that included Hunter, who was by no means a small man.

This must be Levi Barra, Felicity's husband. His shoulders were as broad as a lumberjack's and bulged with strength beneath his coffee-colored waistcoat.

At the sight of her, he moved out from behind the table and approached her with an ambling sort of grace. "Miss Sherrington, I presume?" He held out one enormous paw, which she noted was as scarred and callused as Dodge's hands were. "I am Levi Barra. Welcome to our dinner table."

"Pleased to meet you, sir. Thank you for inviting me." She placed her hand in his, wondering what kind of men owned a diamond mine and still found the need to work their fingers to the bone like the Barras clearly did.

He took his time studying her. "It was entirely my wife's doing, but you are welcome nonetheless."

"She is very kind, sir. I am most grateful."

"Levi," he corrected with a shake of his head. "We Barras don't stand much on ceremony. Wasn't too long ago we were jumping a claim on this place and trying to scrounge up a crop and a herd to call our own.

Jane lowered her hand to her side and relaxed a few degrees. Clearly, there were many shades of the law, and he'd skirted a few of the grayer ones. Well, she wasn't one to throw stones, considering her own spotty past and many sketchy acquaintances.

He returned to the head of the table. "Please be seated." He angled his head at Dodge and seemed to be issuing a silent command.

Without flickering an eyelash, Dodge pulled back a chair for her. For the next few strained moments of silence, Jane was very much aware of the hand he left resting on the high back of her chair. To her enormous relief, Felicity soon bustled through the doorway with a platter of steaming meat and vegetables.

"You look lovely this evening, Jane."

"All the credit goes to you, ma'am. I thank you again for the dress."

Felicity tossed her head as if to downplay her guest's gushing gratitude. "The blue suits her eyes to perfection, don't you think so, Dodge?" Her sparkling gaze sought out her youngest brother-in-law.

Unused to compliments, Jane could hardly breathe as she awaited his response.

He paused for a few heartbeats, then his gravely baritone rumbled deliciously through her. "She's a fetching little chickabiddy, alright."

Oh, my! Jane felt close to swooning. First, he'd called her Jinglebell Jane and now chickabiddy, like a soft, downy chick. For a person who beheld her with such suspicion, he sure had a sizable collection of endearments stored behind that cocky stare of his.

The family seated themselves and reached out to join hands.

When Jane hesitated to take Dodge's hand, he arched a challenging brow at her. She lightly touched her fingers to his, hoping they weren't trembling.

He curled his much larger, much warmer hand around hers and bowed his head.

She did likewise, amazed at how safe she felt within the

four walls of the dining room with Levi's deep voice calmly intoning grace. Normally, dinner time involved a few freshly skinned and grilled squirrels around a campfire. It also tended to involve loud, bawdy, male conversations peppered with expletives and thinly veiled suggestions about how she might keep herself warm the rest of the night.

Despite how suspicious and standoffish Dodge Barra had acted toward her so far, his hold on her hand was gentle. Also, he made no effort to tug her closer while all eyes were closed like a few of her brother's cronies might have if they were present.

She and Dodge did, however, bump elbows and shoulders several times while passing the gravy and biscuits. And every time they bumped, Jane found herself very much aware of the scowling cowboy to her right. She ignored his stiff demeanor and his stubborn refusal to enter the dinner conversation, trying to pretend they had grown up together and were great pals. How she longed for a friend her age!

The pot roast was mouth meltingly delicious, so tender that it fell apart on her tongue. It was all Jane could do not to sigh out loud at how wonderful everything tasted, right down to the blackberry preserves Felicity passed around to spread on the biscuits. Jane knew she was overeating, but she couldn't help it. She'd gone to bed hungry way too many times before.

Felicity more than made up for Dodge's silence, keeping a lively stream of chatter going the entire meal. She waited until Jane laid down her fork before folding her hands and leaning in her direction. "We'd like you to attend school, Jane."

Jane's eyes widened. She glanced around the table to gauge the reaction of the two men present. Levi smiled his encouragement and approval, while Dodge maintained a deadpan expression. "I, er, I don't rightly know how long I'll be staying."

Felicity shrugged. "Understood, my friend, but a few reading and writing lessons won't hurt no matter how long or how short you stay with us."

Jane dropped her gaze, wondering how Felicity had guessed one of Jane's most dark and painful little secrets. Thanks to a harsh and demanding uncle who preferred to have her at home cooking and cleaning, she hadn't attended much in the way of classes since grammar school. Thus, she could only read haltingly and couldn't write much more than her own name. And that hadn't been the worst part of her stint in her uncle's household. The belt he liked to swing at her when he was deep in his cups had been far worse than the endless workload. Sometimes he was so inebriated, he'd swung the wrong end of the belt, bringing the metal buckle down on her shoulders and back. She had the unattractive scars to show for it. So did Hunter. The constant abuses were what had finally broken something inside her brother.

It was a dark and rainy evening, and their guardian had been in a particularly foul mood. He'd launched himself at Jane, swinging a belt in each hand; and Hunter had come unraveled. He'd jumped in front of his sister, wrestled one of the belts away from their uncle, and fought him off until the man collapsed in a drunken stupor it the middle of the floor. That same night, Hunter had snatched up Jane and escaped the horrid household with her beneath the cover of darkness. With little more than the clothes on their backs and the rifle Hunter had helped himself to from their uncle's collection, they initially become street rats with Hunter picking pockets to survive. However, he had soon elevated his ambitions to bigger heists, claiming his sister deserved far better than the poor set of cards they'd been dealt.

"Mind you, we will not force you to attend school, though

we highly encourage it." Felicity's kind voice wrenched Jane back to the present

Jane glanced around the table to find all three of the Barras were studying her with puzzled expressions. Dodge's gaze was resting on her hand, which she hadn't realized was rubbing her shoulder where the worst scar rested beneath the blue velvet of her borrowed gown.

Jane hastily dropped her hand. "I'll attend school, ma'am, if that's what you wish. Do not be surprised if they sit me with the young ones, though. I am dreadfully behind in my studies."

Felicity's smile was full of so much understanding and sympathy that Jane nearly burst into tears again. "Do not worry your pretty head about that, my friend." She beamed a smile across the table at her brother-in-law. "Dodge here has agreed to tutor you."

"He has?" Jane exclaimed, whipping her head in his direction. "That is, what I mean to say is, thank you."

His upper lip curled. "My pleasure," he returned in a tone that narrowly missed being a sneer.

"Well, now that the topic of your education is settled," Felicity clapped her hands in delight, "I promised Levi I'd let him take me to the theater this evening."

In a daze, Jane helped clear the table and positioned herself at the sink to wash dishes so Felicity and Levi could get on the road that much sooner.

"I could get used to having an extra set of hands around here," Felicity trilled as she breezed around the kitchen, putting away the leftover roast and vegetables.

Jane adored how everyone in the household pitched in, even Levi who gathered up the scraps and took them outside to feed the dogs.

"I can take a hint," Dodge growled. He snatched the dish towel away from Felicity when she reached for it and held it high over her head. "I'll dry dishes tonight. You go on and enjoy your show."

She leaned in to kiss his cheek, eliciting a grin of adoration from him.

Well! Jane hid a smile. Looked like the crotchety Dodge had at least one weakness — his lovely sister-in-law.

Felicity disappeared into the hallway, leaving Jane alone with Dodge. She mentally braced herself, fully expecting his forced jovialness to evaporate as soon as his brother and sister-in-law drove away.

Jane wasn't mistaken. With her hands plunged deep in the sink water, she watched their carriage drive down the sandy, well-beaten path leading away from the Barra ranch.

"When is your brother coming back for you?" Dodge's voice low in her ear made her jump and nick her finger on a knife hidden beneath the suds.

"Ow!" She momentarily closed her eyelids against the slice of pain.

"I didn't lay a hand on you!" he declared in indignation, stomping away from her. "I don't know what you're complaining about."

"I didn't say you did." She opened her eyes and watched him stow a stack of plates in the storage cabinet on the other side of the room. When his back was safely turned, she removed her hand from the water and stared at the ooze of red. *Of all the rotten luck!* It was going to require a bandage.

"What in tarnation?" Catching sight of the red, Dodge stomped back in her direction.

"I cut myself on a knife, I think." Feeling a little lightheaded, Jane leaned her elbows on the sink and sucked in a deep breath. "Reckon I can trouble you for anything that can serve as a bandage?"

When he didn't answer, she glanced over her shoulder to discover him gone. The rear door from the kitchen was swinging wide on its hinges. A large, orange-haired cat sidled into the kitchen, stared at her a moment through unblinking eyes, and issued a sharp meow of protest.

Jane chuckled despite her wooziness. "I imagine you want to know who I am and what I've done with your mistress, little one."

He meowed again and trotted a few steps closer.

"Are you looking for scraps?" she crooned. "I fear you might be out of luck, my little furry friend, since the dogs already helped themselves to everything we scraped off the plates."

He purred and came close enough to butt his head against the toe of her boot.

"Is that a hug? Because I could really use a hug about now," Jane sighed, wondering where Dodge had gone.

She didn't have to wonder long. He stomped back into the kitchen with two handfuls of supplies — a pair of scissors, a needle and thread, and a roll of white cloth. "Oh!" She shot him a grateful look. "For a minute there, I thought you'd abandoned me."

He snorted and cast a concerned look at her finger. "Why don't you dunk it back under the water, so I can see what we're dealing with?"

She complied and came up with a dripping forefinger that quickly turned red again as more blood oozed.

He reached for her wrist and turned her hand this way and that to examine it more closely. "You shouldn't ever put the dinner knives down in the water. Haven't you washed dishes before?"

Jane couldn't possibly explain her life on the road to him, so she bit her lip. "Are you going to help me or just stand there lecturing?" She sucked in a breath as he dunked her hand again and patted it dry with a short length he cut from the white bandage roll. The blood letting didn't slow one bit.

"It needs stitches." It wasn't a question. It was an emphatic statement. Dodge let go of her wrist long enough to remove his dinner jacket and roll up his sleeves. He proceeded to wash his hands and the needle.

"What? I thought you were a rancher and a mine owner," she muttered through gritted teeth, eyeing the sharp silver needle. "Are you a doctor, too?"

"I've learned to be a little of everything." He reached for her hand once more. "In the past, we couldn't afford to go blubbering to a doctor every time we got a cut or scratch. We can afford it now, but why bother? I can get you all fixed up in a fraction of the time it would take to drive you across town and wake up the doc."

Jane's lips parted. "You would do that for me? That is, drive me all the way across town?" She and Dodge barely knew each other; and the vibes he was sending off didn't make her feel like he held her in very high esteem…not that she blamed him.

"You sound worried, chickabiddy. I'm here, aren't I?"

"Wielding a sharp object," she affirmed with a shaky laugh.

He held the needle suspended over her hand. "Well, what's it to be, your highness?" he drawled sarcastically, "Surgeon Dodge Barra or a trip across town?"

She rolled her eyes at him. "Since you asked so nicely, I should probably give you the benefit of the doubt."

He didn't delay any longer. He plunged the needle in the pad of her finger and sewed the first stitch.

It wasn't that Jane was overly fearful of a few stitches, but the sight of blood had always unnerved her; and tonight there was so much of it.

"Think of something pleasant, chickabiddy," Dodge urged huskily. "It'll be over soon. Just a stitch or two more."

Jane closed her eyes and turned her face away, swallowing hard. "Why are you being nice to me?"

He sniffed. "Answer my question first. Then I'll answer yours."

"Y-your question?" she stuttered. *Oh, right.* "You wanted to know when Hunter is coming back for me."

"That I do, seeing as your presence here could very well put us all in danger."

"He won't hurt you," she protested, incensed that Dodge would assume such. "You don't know the first thing about my brother. He's not like that."

"There's a trail of bodies across the west that says otherwise, chickabiddy."

"He only shoots in self defense. He never draws first."

"Is that so?"

"That's a second question," she noted dryly. "I only agreed to answer one. Then you get to answer mine."

"Fair enough. I'm still waiting." He tied off the thread, cut it, and swabbed away the rest of the blood. Then he proceeded to roll the bandage around her finger, enclosing the stitches in a soft white cloth.

"I don't know. That's the same answer I gave the sheriff to his long lists of questions, and it's the truth. I don't know anything, Dodge. My brother always keeps his own council. He doesn't consult me. He doesn't give me advance notice of his heists. He doesn't take me with him when he goes. He doesn't tell me how long he'll be gone or when he'll return. At this exact moment, I do not know if he is dead or alive." She stopped and drew a deep, shuddery breath.

"Very well. To answer your question, I wouldn't sit around and watch any creature suffer, not even an old farm critter like Mr. Fussy Pants here."

"Mr. Fussy Pants!" she exclaimed with a chuckle. What a name!

"The cat," he supplied dryly, "meaning I would've offered to stitch you up, regardless."

"Regardless of my last name, you mean." Her voice came out more bitter than she intended.

He secured the bandage and released her hand. "How about I finish cleaning up in here, and we'll start your first reading lesson in the parlor, seeing as you might not fancy holding a pen this evening?"

"You're all heart." She had no choice but to do his bidding, since finishing the dishes would dampen the bandage he'd worked so meticulously to apply.

"I reckon I have you fooled." He offered her the ghost of a smile that did crazy things to her heart.

CHAPTER 4: SCHOOLING

DODGE

*D*odge wasn't overly proud of the fact, but he found himself actually enjoying his tutoring sessions with Jane throughout the next week. She was eager to learn and sponged up every ounce of knowledge she could. By the end of the first week, she was reading short, simple sentences in a halting voice.

Alas, he was no closer to figuring out the answer to his most burning question — when was Hunter coming back to fetch his sister?

Though he watched Jane closely, even paying an impromptu visit to the schoolhouse during lunchtime on Friday, Dodge had not observed anything to shed light on Jane's involvement with her brother's crime spree. In fact, it was starting to look like she might actually be telling the truth about her utter lack of involvement, which was difficult to wrap his brain around. How was it possible that Hunter Sherrington had committed so many crimes while keeping his sister's hands clean of them all?

"Did you stop by the school to spy on me, Investigator

Dodge?" Jane asked without preamble, when he sidled up to her at the edge of the school grounds.

He glanced around them, immediately noting she was sitting alone with her lunch pail in her lap. "Aw, is that your way of saying you were missing me and yearning for a bit of my engaging company, chickabiddy?" He plopped down beside her, unconcerned about getting grass stains on his denim trousers, and stretched his legs out in front of him. It felt good to get off his feet, since he'd been supervising a shift down at the mine all morning. They were cutting a new tunnel, and he was overseeing it.

"Why do you always answer my questions with another question?" she fumed, scowling prettily up at him.

"Now that, my little Miss Jinglebell Jane, is yet another question," he pointed out. "Isn't that the pot calling the kettle black?"

She let out a tiny moan of frustration as she bit fiercely into her sandwich, a sound he found utterly entrancing.

To his intense irritation, his stomach chose that moment to growl — loudly.

She lowered her sandwich and stared at him while she finished chewing. Her finger was much better, though she still had a light bandage on to cover her stitches. "When was the last time you ate?"

"I eat all the time." His stomach growled again. He ignored it and rolled to his back, folding his arms behind his head as he stared up at the sky. After a moment, he closed his eyes. Man, but it felt good to take a load off for a few minutes!

"That's not an answer. Here." Something tickled his nose. Something that smelled heavenly.

Dodge opened his eyes to discover Jane had torn off half her sandwich and was dangling it directly over his nose — meat, bread, and all. He weakly swatted at her hand. "I don't want to take your lunch. You need to eat, too. You're barely more than skin and bones."

She grimaced. "Hmm, I imagine that silver tongue of yours is mighty popular with the ladies."

He closed his eyes again, not caring what anyone else thought of him, male or female. Most folks' opinions quite simply didn't interest him. His mind drifted, and he was close to nodding off when something brushed his lips. Drat Jane and her sandwich! She didn't give a fellow a chance to take the high road, and he only had so much willpower where his stomach was concerned. Without thinking, he reached up and closed his hand around her wrist to hold the sandwich in place while he took a bite.

And thought he died and went to Heaven...

It was more of Felicity's famous pot roast, a thick juicy slice of it sandwiched between two pieces of fresh baked oat and honey bread.

"Dodge!" Jane hissed. "Let go of my hand. We're in the process of receiving a very disapproving look from my teacher."

He opened his eyes and swiped the rest of the sandwich from between her fingers. "Callie Barra is kin, one of my sister-in-laws, to be precise. What is she going to do to me?"

Jane's gaze spit indignant blue flames. "I'm more concerned about what she's going to do to *me*!"

"Janey has a beau! Janey has a beau!" one of the younger girls on the playground chanted. Dodge glanced in surprise in the child's direction, eliciting a round of giggles from her and her circle of friends. All four of them ran off arm-in-arm.

"Oh, dear!" Jane moaned. "Now look what you've done."

Dodge pushed up on one elbow to face Jane as he polished off the half of sandwich she'd shared with him. "I did some asking around about you. That's how I found out about all the shunning you're facing here at school. Maybe that's the real reason I stopped by today."

It wasn't, but he was enjoying baiting Jane. He eyed her closely and felt a surge of manly pleasure when her cheeks turned pink.

"Dodge Barra! Sometimes I just don't know about you."

"Good!" He winked at her. "See? Never a dull moment around me. I'm just full of excitement."

"You're full of something, alright," she grumbled, glancing around them from beneath her lashes. "Stuff and nonsense, that's what."

"Janey has a beau!" Another child chanted softly as she dashed past them.

"I'm never going to live this down," Jane bit her lower lip, "and neither are you."

He shrugged, sitting up. "Well, at least we gave them something else to talk about other than your relationship to Hunter Sherrington."

Jane shook her head. "You really want your name paired with the sister of a wanted criminal?" she asked fiercely. Her face turned a bright pink, and her eyes misted with tears.

"A most wanted criminal, at that," he corrected in a saucy tone, hating how distressed she looked. He leaned forward to tap her on the nose with a finger. "Not just any old criminal."

Jane's breathing hitched, and she made a sound that could have been a chuckle or a sob; he wasn't sure which. "Your family deserves better than to have their good name mucked up with mine. It's bad enough that I'm staying out at your ranch. You really don't have to make a public show of being nice to me. I don't need your sympathy, nor do I want it." With that, she stuffed her sandwich wrapping in her lunch pail, dusted off her skirts, and stood. Today, she was wearing a red wine-colored wool dress he found almost as fetching as the blue velvet one.

Dodge let himself revel for a moment in Jane's show of temper. She was pretty all hours of the day. When she was angry, however, she was stunning. He liked that about her. She had pluck and spirit. Plus, she was turning out to be one of the kindest, most generous souls he'd ever encountered. Something in his gut told him it wouldn't have mattered how hungry she was or how little food she'd brought along. She would have shared it, anyway.

"Dodge Barra!" a woman exclaimed in a none-too-happy voice.

With an inward groan, Dodge curled himself to his feet and dusted the grass from his trousers. He took his place beside Jane. It was time to face the general. "Yes, ma'am." He straightened like a soldier and popped a sharp salute to Callie Barra. Tennyson's wife was a fiery red-head with a temper to match and she looked ready to boil over on them. He could only hope her ice blue silk gown would cool her anger a few degrees.

Her hands were fisted on her slender hips, and she was wearing her most teacherfied expression. "You can't just march onto my playground and break all the rules now that you've graduated."

"Rules?" He pretended innocence. "Oh, no, ma'am. I wouldn't dream of breaking any rules."

Jane made a snorting sound at his shoulder. "You're going to pay for this," she hissed.

"Oh? Do you have something to add to the conversation, Miss Sherrington?" Callie demanded sharply.

"No, ma'am," she mumbled in a miserable voice.

Yes, indeed, Dodge was going to die a slow, painful death later that evening. He rather looked forward to the encounter.

"Good. How about you end your lunch early and go

inside to write out Proverbs 11:22 twenty times on a sheet of paper?"

"You said Proverbs 11:22, ma'am?" Jane sounded so mortified it was all Dodge could do not to reach for her hand.

"I did, and do you have that scripture memorized, Miss Sherrington?" Callie continued coolly.

"No, ma'am. I do not believe so."

"I thought not. Well, you will shortly. It says, *as a ring of gold in a swine's snout, so is a beautiful woman who lacks discretion.*"

Dodge muffled a laugh. Oh, he was so going to pay for this, but he was enjoying every second of it while he still lived and breathed.

"Oh," Jane replied faintly. "Y-you think I'm beautiful, Mrs. Barra?"

"For your impertinence, you can write it thirty times, now, Miss Sherrington."

"Oh, ma'am, I am so sorry. Truly I am! I didn't mean—"

"Fifty times, Miss Sherrington. Are you quite finished talking back?"

Jane nodded, her cheeks a mottled shade of horrified. With one last furious glance at Dodge, she ran for the schoolhouse.

"That was cruel," Dodge noted, trying not to laugh.

"It was necessary!" Callie snapped. "Little pitchers have big ears, and I've a reputation to maintain around here." She glanced around them. "Walk with me."

She led them away from the schoolhouse to the edge of the school grounds. "You need to leave. Now."

"If you insist," he returned in an agreeable voice.

"And don't come back." She shot a worried glance over her shoulder and tucked a loose strand of hair behind her ear. "Jane is having enough trouble as it is. She doesn't need you making things worse for her."

He scowled down at his sister-in-law. "What sort of trouble?"

She shrugged and folded her arms. "It's because of who she is. What else? Children can be cruel, and these miner families want nothing to do with her. They mock her. They call her names."

He waggled his brows at his sister-in-law. "And now they can claim Dodge Barra is courting her."

Callie gave him an incredulous look. "Doesn't that bother you?" Her expression turned speculative. "Wait! Did you plan this?"

"No," he answered honestly, "but I didn't do anything to stop it, either." He jammed his hands in his pockets. "I had my suspicions about Jane, at first. Ah, maybe I still do, but I'm starting to hope I'm wrong about her."

"What sort of suspicions?" Callie hugged her middle as if suddenly cold.

Dodge clenched his jaw. "I think the rumors are true. I think her brother is coming for her. No idea when or how, but he's coming. What I don't yet know is if she'll be complicit when he does."

"Tennyson says much the same thing," his sister-in-law confided. She lowered her voice. "Ten made me start carrying a pistol in my reticule, just in case."

"So you'll keep an eye on Jane for me?" he asked anxiously.

"For you?" She grimaced and shook her head. "Is that the way the wind is blowing between the two of you, then?"

He huffed out a breath. Callie's skepticism was understandable. He'd only known Jane a week, yet already he was growing possessive of her. Did that mean he was holding a candle for the lass? It was hard to say. He'd never felt this way about a person of the female persuasion before. "If you must know, then yes. I think she's special, Callie, and I'd just as soon that bit of information *not* get back to Tennyson just yet, please and thank you. Or to Levi and Prescott."

"Oh, Dodge," she wailed softly. "I don't keep secrets from Ten and certainly not something this important. You're so young, and the Sherringtons are, well, so…dangerous. I don't want to see you get hurt in any way. None of us do."

"She's but seventeen, Callie, and she hasn't had it easy most of those seventeen years."

"Sure and a lot of young women are married by that age and bearing children," Callie shot back.

"Even so, she's been through a lot. Can't you cut her a little slack?" He recalled the scars Felicity said were riddled across Jane's shoulders and back. Maybe it was time they all gave her the benefit of the doubt.

"I don't rightly know what to do, Dodge." Callie glanced over her shoulder again. "Listen, I have to get back to the schoolhouse. It's time for our afternoon lessons."

"Fine. You do what you think you have to do, and I'll face whatever fallout comes of it." He planted his feet firmly on the ground. "However, I'm not budging until you promise to keep an eye on Jane. That's all that really matters." He'd gladly take a scolding or two or three from his brothers for it later.

"I already told you about the pistol, Dodge. What more do you want?"

"Your promise to protect her as fiercely as you would any other student should any harm come her way."

"But of course!" She looked aghast at his request and a little offended.

"Promise me," he snarled, not willing to take any chances.

"It's not necessary, but I promise," she said sharply. Then she spun around and left him in a swirl of blue skirts.

Dodge stared after her, wishing he'd not been so crass with his sister-in-law. He wasn't entirely certain why he was feeling so twitchy today. He glanced up at the sky and scowled at the clouds rolling over the sun. It was turning overcast. In another part of the country, it might spell rain; but it rarely rained in Headstone, Arizona. They were too far into the desert. It was more likely that a sand storm would blow in, as anything else.

For reasons he didn't delve into too deeply, Dodge found himself lingering in Hope's Landing, though he normally would have headed home this time of day to help out with the horses. He fiddled with some paperwork at the mining office until his half-sister, Madge, ran him off.

"What's gotten into you today?" she scolded.

"I'm just trying to be helpful," he retorted, wondering why everyone always insisted on treating him like a pesky fly to be swatted out of the way. Sure, he was the youngest Barra brother, but he was eighteen now. A man in his own right. Part owner of a diamond mine. A fairly successful bull rider, though Prescott had already set all the records in the family. Dodge did his fair share of the work, earned his fair share of the pay, and was past ready for his siblings to start acting like it!

"Well, I've got this paperwork the way I want it, and I prefer that no one else touches it." Madge smoothed her hands over her already smooth salt and pepper bun to ensure no hairs were out of place. She gave her skirts a hearty flounce to settle them around her knees behind her desk.

Dodge muffled a snort. There were never any hairs out of place on Madge. She was neat as a pin and so painfully tidy that he was half tempted to muss her hair on his way out the door. However, Madge had been like a second mother to him after their mother had passed. He wouldn't put it past her to pull out a switch and come after him if he did something so reckless.

He pulled out his pocket watch to check the time. It was a gift from their father, whom they all somewhat affectionately called Old Mack. The old geezer had more or less lost the right to be called their father shortly after their mother died. He'd kicked all four of his sons out of their mountain home, forcing them out into the world to fend for themselves while he remained alone on the mountain to grieve. Though Levi had finally talked him into moving to their ranch in Head-stone, Old Mack insisted on living in one of the cabins behind the main ranch house that would normally be reserved for the hired help. They rarely saw hide or hair of him.

"Still carrying that old watch around?" Madge mused in a gentler voice. "I'm surprised it still works."

Dodge shoved it back in his pocket. "I like old things. Don't have to worry about messing them up." It was nearly time to go "accidentally" bump into Jane on her walk home from school.

"Are you certain you're feeling alright?" she inquired, her tone waxing all preachy again. "You seem a little unlike your-self today."

"I'm worried about Jane," he admitted. "Her brother is coming for her."

Madge looked amazed. "Of course he is! Word on the street is she's the only person in the world who matters to him. I'm more worried about MaryAnne Branson, though. Stands to reason, Hunter will blame her for his sister's arrest, when it's all said and done."

"Maybe. Guess I figured that's MaryAnne's brothers' problem." MaryAnne had two brothers, Colt and Jordan. As far as Dodge was concerned, it was their job to worry about MaryAnne, while he and the rest of the Barra brothers worried about Jane. For reasons Dodge still didn't understand, Felicity had decided to make Jane the Barras' problem. She'd made noises about visiting the girl in jail and being impressed by her grit. Felicity had also spent a decent amount of time behind closed doors with MaryAnne, since the Bransons had chosen her as their sister's attorney when the case against Hunter Sherrington finally went to court. Then again, Hunter Sherrington had to be arrested first.

"Aren't you a cold, unfeeling creature today?" Madge studied him in amazement.

"I prefer the term practical." Dodge moved towards the door of his half-sister's tiny office.

"A Barra brother through and through," she sighed, giving him a loving but shrewd look. "I reckon it's about time for school to let out for the day."

He chuckled. "Not much gets past you, does it Mama Madge?"

"Not much," she agreed, eyes twinkling. "Are you properly armed, just in case?"

"Is the sky blue?" he countered, pushing open the door.

"Not so much today," she shot back. "Looks like a storm is headed our way. Do you have an umbrella?"

"Is the sky blue?" he said again with a smirk. Of course he didn't have an umbrella.

This time, they both laughed.

"Get on with you, then." Madge winked at him. "Everyone knows you're too mean to melt."

"I love you, too, Madge." With a mock salute, Dodge took off at a jog down the street.

The school house was only a few blocks away. Jane was sauntering out the front door and skipping down the steps when he arrived.

She took one look at him hanging over the fence gate and rolled her eyes. "You again, huh?"

"Me, again," he affirmed, falling into step beside her when she exited the school grounds.

"I reckon you don't think you got me into enough trouble for the day already?" she fumed.

"Janey's got a beau!" some child shrieked near his elbow and took off at a sprint, as if expecting a good chase.

"Good gravy!" Dodge exclaimed. "Please assure me you didn't have to listen to that all afternoon."

"I can't offer that assurance," she snapped. "May we change the subject, please?"

"Sure. I was actually thinking I should just go ahead and kiss you to get it over with," he taunted. He was fine with moving on to the next subject.

"Kiss me!" She stumbled, and he reached out to steady her arm. "Whatever for?"

He shot her an innocent look. "You tell me. You're the one who wrote about how beautiful you are a good fifty times this afternoon."

She lifted her chin. "You're a heartless cad!"

"A cad who very much wishes to kiss you."

She made a furious hissing sound. "Again, why? Have you ever kissed a girl before, Dodge?"

"No." He saw no point in lying about something so important.

"Oh." Her voice came out breathless. "I reckon you're curious about what it feels like, then?"

He was amused and charmed at how utterly un-missish she was about discussing the topic. "Not exactly." He shot her a sideways glance, feeling the heat crawl up his neck. "I just want to know what it's like to kiss you."

"Oh," she sighed. "You know, for a cad, you sure have a way of making a girl feel special."

"Good, because you are special." He was starting to feel mighty pleased with himself.

"Cocky," she muttered, making him want to kiss her all the more.

He admired her pluck and adored her sass all the more for how much she'd suffered in the past. Her spirit was living proof of the inner strength she'd developed along the way. It was something he could relate to, something they had in common.

"I reckon you'll want to kiss a few girls, so you have someone to compare me to?" she mused in an irritated voice.

He scowled down at her. "Nope. Can't think of anyone else I want to kiss." They walked past a copse of trees. By now, all the other children had long since gone their separate ways. Most of them lived on Miner's Row right there in Hope's Landing. "I reckon you're asking so many questions, because you've never kissed a fellow before, either?"

"I wish I hadn't," she confessed in a small voice, then clapped a hand over her mouth.

He reached for her lunch pail in order to have something to do with his hands, since he suddenly wanted to plow a fist through the nearest tree trunk. "Did someone hurt you, chickabiddy?"

"No. It was just a young, foolish robber who lost his head one night when the boys were celebrating."

"I see, and did your brother find out?" He hoped Hunter had thrown him into a river, better yet, over a waterfall.

"The fool kissed me in full view of my brother, who promptly socked him a good one on the noggin and cut him loose from the gang." She shook her head. "He begged to be reinstated, but my brother showed no mercy. No one ever dared touch me again."

"I'm beginning to like your brother."

To his shock, Jane made a little gasping sound and pulled on his hand, tugging him into the tree line.

"What are you doing, little chickabiddy?" He smirked down at her.

"This." She stood on her tiptoes to brush her lips against his.

His heart pounded a thousand beats a minute as her soft, warm mouth moved against his. He suddenly felt like he could slay dragons and move mountains. He wanted to hold his Jinglebell Jane so tightly that no harm could ever reach her again. He never wanted to let her go. Then again, he didn't want to come across as a groping, fumbling fool; so he kept his arms at his sides.

Jane stepped closer and touched her fingertips to his cheek. "Normally, a fellow puts his arms around his girl when they're kissing," she whispered.

"Like this?" he muttered, hooking his one free arm around her waist and drew her against his chest, which felt scandalously amazing. He still held her lunch pail in his other hand.

"Exactly like that. Kiss me again, Dodge."

"I haven't kissed you yet, chickabiddy," he teased. "That was all you the first time around."

She rolled her eyes and started to pull back, but he tightened his arm around her and tugged her closer. He slowly lowered his mouth to hers, keeping his eyes on hers the whole time. He'd watched his brother, Tennyson, kiss Callie this way; and he'd been dying to try it ever since. Well, someday, at least, when he met the right girl. Like Jane.

This time, Jane sighed and wrapped her arms around his neck, melting into him.

Dodge's heart leaped at the thought that Tennyson's kissing technique was a winning one. He'd be sure to thank him later. In the end, it didn't matter that Dodge had never kissed a girl before, because he instinctively knew exactly how to kiss his Jane. Inside his head, he was reeling in shock and awe. So *this* was what had brought his three older brothers to their knees the last two years, as one-by-one they'd met the loves of their lives.

A distant shot being fired had Dodge yanking his head up. He pushed Jane behind him and drew his pistol from the holster hidden beneath his shirt.

Seeing nothing but sand, cacti, and tumbleweeds for miles, he shook his head. There were canyons and mesas in the distance, but they were way too far away for someone to be firing from them.

Three more shots were fired in quick succession. Then silence ensued.

"Could be a hunter, I reckon," Dodge muttered, "but it doesn't sound right or feel right."

"I think it's a signal," Jane blurted, sounding distressed. "I think Hunter is back in town."

CHAPTER 5: COMING STORM

JANE

"*L*et's get you home," Dodge said tersely.

To Jane's delight, he reached for her hand. She had to switch her pistol from one hand to the other to clasp his.

He scowled at her handgun. "Where did you get that?"

"From Levi and Felicity, since you insist on being so nosy."

His lips twitched. "Are you a good shot?"

She grimaced. "If you say *for a girl*, I'll be sorely tempted to wing you."

"Do not worry, chickabiddy, I am very, very glad you're a girl."

The look on his face made her catch her breath. "Name your target, and I'll shoot it."

Humor glinted deep in his mocking eyes that she was coming to adore so much. He pointed. "That yonder cactus with the mole-like protrusion on the side."

She aimed and fired at the mole, blasting it off the side of the cactus. "There. I think it looks better now. Agreed?"

"Forget the cactus! I think I just fell in love with you." He

54

looked so sweetly indulgent that it was all Jane could do not to throw herself back in his arms. However, she was convinced Hunter was out there somewhere nearby. It was best to return to the Barra ranch before he made himself known.

Jane raised her brows at Dodge. "You fancy yourself in love with me, because I shot a mole off a fool cactus?"

"Most definitely because of that," he assured in a tender voice that made her heart race, "and because you are kind and generous, the most beautiful person I ever met on the inside and the outside, not to mention the world's best kisser."

She wrinkled her nose at him. "I thought I was the only girl you ever kissed."

He held up a tanned finger over her lunch pail. "Exactly, and I confess I already want to kiss you again."

"Dodge," she sighed. "I adore you so much. I truly do, but my brother is coming for me. We both know that. We've always known that."

"Well, I've decided he can't have you." His jaw clenched. "I know the two of you are kin, so I don't mind sharing you with him; but I'll not let him take you away for good."

Hope leaped into Jane's chest. In that moment, she wanted so badly to believe Dodge. "I do not know what to say, and I cannot make any promises right now."

"Can't or won't," he taunted, "because I have an idea."

"You do?" Jane squeezed his hand. "Please share."

"It's simple. Your brother loves you more than anything, which means he'll only want what's best for you."

"And..." she prodded when Dodge fell silent.

"I'm what's best for you, chickabiddy." He bent down to kiss the top of her head. "All we have to do is convince him of that."

"How?" she cried, desperately wanting to believe him.

"I must warn you. There's a diamond involved."

"A diamond," she repeated slowly, throat constricting as the possibilities flooded her brain.

"A ring, to be precise."

"You want me to..." Her voice dwindled shyly. She was unable to finish the sentence.

"Marry you, yes." He squeezed her hand.

"I'm still in school, Dodge." She could barely choke out the words.

"Some day, when you're ready, then. There's no rush for us to get married," he assured huskily. "Levi is busy deeding off a piece of property for me. When I finally have the deed in hand, I can start building you a house."

"Build me a house!" she exclaimed, snapping her fingers in the air. "Just like that?" She couldn't imagine having so much money at one's disposal.

He nodded. "I can afford it. You'll just need to sketch out how many rooms you want and where you want me to put them, that sort of thing."

"Oh, Dodge!" She gripped his hand tightly. "Believe me, when I say I want this. I want it so badly it hurts. I want everything you talked about — to be married, to live in a beautiful house. I want respectability and to be on the right side of the law again. I want it all, but mostly I just want you, and that terrifies me." Tears prickled behind her eyelids, making her want to moan in frustration. Ever since she'd met Dodge and his family, she'd turned into a downright watering pot. If she wasn't careful, they were going to think she was some weeping ninny.

They reached the perimeter of the Barra property, and Dodge paused their march to the house. Since she was still holding his hand, it forced her to pause, as well. He turned her to face him squarely. "I'm not asking for any promises yet, chickabiddy, though I will be asking for them soon. I just need to know one thing. When your brother comes for you, will you choose to stay with me?"

That was the question burning a hole in her heart right now. Would Hunter give her a choice? They'd been through so much together; and, as wrong as he was in the path he'd chosen, he'd done it all for her. Though he rarely discussed anything of importance with her concerning his crimes, Hunter had been clear about one thing. He had a stash of money saved up somewhere, and he was planning to use it to settle down and give her a normal life...eventually. But that was the problem with Hunter. With him, it was never going to be over. She feared he was too damaged to ever settle down now, his heart too stained with sin. There would always be one more heist.

"I don't know if Hunter will give me a choice," she warned softly.

"Make him." Dodge tipped her chin up with a single finger. "From what I know of Hunter Sherrington, it's the only way you and I can ever hope to be together. There's no running away from this. No avoiding what's coming. You'll have to face him and talk it out. You know I'm right."

Jane gulped and nodded. After years of being a loner, she'd found Dodge, and it was like he could read her thoughts. He could see right through her. He understood her. "How did you get to be so wise?"

"Through hard times, chickabiddy."

She reached up to touch his cheek. "I love being your chickabiddy, Dodge, and your Jinglebell Jane." She offered him a tremulous smile. "No one ever gave me nicknames before. I know you're just being silly when you call me those names, but it makes me feel special."

"Well, I happen to love being your heartless cad," he

57

teased, making light of one of the few nicknames she'd given him.

She blushed hard. "I reckon I better come up with a few sweet nothings, so you won't throw that back in my face the rest of our lives."

He leaned in to rest his forehead against hers. "Fire away. I'm ready."

"Now?" she chuckled. "You want me to come up with a new nickname for you right now?"

"Why wait?" He touched his lips to hers.

"I can't think straight when you do that," she protested, but her lips melted against his.

"Think crookedly, then." He kissed her again.

She snickered against his mouth. "I've never laughed, cried, and smiled so much in all my life as I have since I met you."

"You make me happy, too, chickabiddy."

A crack of thunder sounded overhead, making them both jolt.

Dodge kissed her again, more lingeringly this time. "We'd best get inside before the storm hits. I'm thinking we may be in for a bit of rain, after all."

THEY MADE A RUN FOR IT, reaching the porch as the first raindrops pelted down. Dodge released Jane's hand before they entered the front door. He had her pass ahead of him.

Felicity was waiting for them at the base of the stairs. "There you are." She looked greatly relieved. "I was so hoping the two of you would make it home before the storm hit."

"As you can see, we are fine." Dodge kissed his sister-in-law's cheek. "Is Levi home yet?"

Felicity's mouth tightened. "He came home and left again.

There were some shots fired earlier that has several of the men in town in a lather. It's probably nothing, but they're worried about everything from poachers to an invading posse from below the border."

"How many ranch hands are still here?" Though Levi offered housing on his ranch, Dodge knew some of the workers returned to homes off site after hours.

"Just the three that live here permanently. Why?"

"No particular reason." Dodge shot Jane a warning glance over his sister-in-law's head. He didn't want to worry Felicity with his fears that Hunter might show up soon on their doorstep. "Just checking on everyone before the storm hits. And Old Mack?"

She made a face. "He's making himself scarce as usual, but I imagine he's in his cabin."

"I'll pay him a quick visit and see if I can get him to stay in the house for a spell this evening." Dodge moved down the hallway towards the back of the house.

"Do you know something about this storm that I don't know?" Felicity called after him anxiously.

"I'm still hoping most of it will blow over," Dodge called back and pushed his way outside. The winds were picking up, and thunder rumbled in the distance. It would be the perfect night for Hunter to stir up mischief. The noise of the storm and the cover of the coming darkness would work in his favor.

Because of the shots fired earlier and Jane's warning, Dodge fully expected that tonight would be the night.

He hurried out the back door and sprinted for Old Mack's cabin, trying not to get soaked through and through. It was a one-room log structure with a wood stove, a bed, and the basic necessities with no extra frills. Levi had argued long and hard with him about moving into the main ranch house, but Old Mack continued to refuse the offer, insisting he needed his own pot of water to boil and his own air to breathe. Dodge figured he'd been roughing it on his own for so long, the old man simply wasn't able to adjust to the more modern comforts of life.

Dodge strode across the narrow covered porch in four long strides to pound on the front door. "Are you inside, Old Mack? There's a storm coming." No one came to the door. He jiggled the handle and found it locked. With a growl of irritation, he tried to peer through the front window, but the glass was shut, and the curtains were drawn.

A rumble of thunder made him glance up at the darkening sky. "Come on, Old Mack," he shouted. "Open up! I'm taking you up to the house to wait it out there." He circled around to the back of his father's home, getting utterly drenched in the process, and jiggled the back door handle. To his surprise, it swung open right away. That was when Dodge realized he was staring down the barrel of a gun.

Though his pulse quickened with a healthy amount of dread, he'd sort of been expecting something like this.

"Come on in, cowboy." Hunter Sherrington spoke with a southern drawl. He was blonde like his sister, possessed striking ice-blue eyes, and was surprisingly not enormous like the rumors and legends had painted him. He boasted a medium height and build, but there was nothing average about the silver revolver in his hand. There was a strange extension on the barrel of his gun that Dodge had never seen before, though he'd heard about such contraptions. It was a handmade silencer. If Hunter chose to fire on him, no one would hear the shot.

Dodge stepped inside the one-room cabin and hastily glanced around. "Where's my father?" The room appeared empty, except for the two of them. "What have you done with him?"

"Well, all that depends on you, son." Hunter waved his

revolver to indicate Dodge should have a seat in the high-back chair he'd dragged to the center of the room.

Dodge sat down, but he didn't wait for Hunter to keep talking. It was time for Dodge to take control of the conversation. "I'm in love with your sister. I want to marry her some day when she's ready."

Hunter froze for a moment. Then he backhanded Dodge with the butt of his gun.

"You can't beat it out of me," Dodge snarled. "I'm the right man for her."

Hunter grimaced. "What do you know about love? You're just a kid."

Dodge ignored the insult. "I can't take the scars off her back, but I can spend the rest of my life trying to remove them from her heart."

Hunter plowed a fist into his gut. "Have you seen her scars, boy?"

"No," Dodge wheezed. "I've only heard about them."

"Aw, have you two kissed, then?"

"For the first time today, sir." Dodge was finding it difficult to breathe and wondered if the last punch had collapsed a lung or something. "I told her I love her, asked her to marry me, and I'm already sketching up plans to build a house for us."

"With what?" Hunter roared. "It takes money to build houses."

"I'm part owner of a diamond mine. I run it with my brothers and the Donovans over at Hope's Landing. I also ride bulls now and then at the local rodeos. I've earned some solid coin that way. I can provide a good living for your sister and any children the good Lord blesses us with."

Hunter's next punch was more vicious than the last. "Already thinking about bedding her, eh?"

Dodge wisely kept his silence. He wasn't capable of much more speech at the moment, anyway.

"If I agree to your request, there will be no more bull riding for you. My sister deserves better."

The next punch rendered Dodge senseless, and his world went black.

CHAPTER 6: FAMILY REUNION

*T*he longer Dodge remained outside, the more anxious Jane grew. Something wasn't right.

"Come join me in the parlor," Felicity urged from the front room. "I just made us a fresh pot of tea and lit some candles."

"I'll be there in a moment," Jane called up the hallway, glancing outside through the back kitchen window again. She could make out Old Mack's cabin from her vantage point, but she could see no sign of Dodge. The front porch was empty and the door and windows closed. He must have gone inside already. Strange how she couldn't see the light of any candles or lanterns through the front curtains.

The sound of a pianoforte drifted down the hallway as Felicity crooned out a melody to match the storm. It was a song full of sobbing notes and minor keys.

Jane's anxiety reached an angsty peak. *I should go check on him, myself.* It wouldn't take that long. Just a few quick steps down the walkway separating the main house from Old Mack's cabin. It would take no more than three to five minutes of her time, tops!

Her mind made up, Jane cracked open the back door and quietly let herself out. No sooner did she shut the door behind her than a crack of thunder rent the air. *Mercy!* She sprinted across the yard, wishing Levi had made it back home already. She hated that he'd left home because of the warning shots fired. She'd recognized those shots, though she'd not confessed the full details to Dodge. It meant another heist was about to take place. It wouldn't have done any good to say anything, though. When Hunter made plans, they were usually foolproof, although it might not look like it at the moment with most of his partners in crime sitting in a jail cell.

In her heart, Jane knew her brother wasn't just coming for her. He was coming for all of those who'd been captured, and that included MaryAnne Branson. Jane was fearful for MaryAnne's life, since she'd betrayed them to the law.

"Dodge, where are you?" she cried, reaching Old Mack's house and banging on the front door.

To her surprise, it opened and someone whisked her inside. She found herself clasped her in a tight hug. "Dodge!" she cried joyfully, but the feel of the man's arms was all wrong — familiar, yet wrong. "Hunter?" she asked in a hesitating tone. "Is it really you?" But she already knew the answer to that.

He held her at arm's length in the dim room. "You knew I would come for you. I'll always come for you. We're family, and family sticks together."

"Yes," she gasped, struggling to step back enough to read his expression. "Yes, I always knew you would come."

His grip tightened on her shoulders, holding her in place. "What on earth did you tell the sheriff to buy your freedom?"

"N-nothing!" she protested, scowling up at him. "What would I tell anyone, at any rate? I know nothing, because you share nothing with me. It's always been that way. Again and again, you shut me out."

Hunter grimaced and set her aside. "I kept you in the dark to protect you. You know that. All my men know that." He paced the small room. "What you don't know cannot incriminate you. I'd just as soon never see you dangling from a hangman's noose."

"As much as I appreciate that, we can't continue on like this forever." Jane's eyesight slowly adjusted to the dimly lit room, but it wasn't enough to make out much more than the shape of a bed and a few odds and ends. "I'm nearly eighteen. I'm growing up. The Barras enrolled me in school."

"So I heard." His voice was bitter. "Is that what you really want, Jane? A normal life with a fenced-in yard and a lapdog? Because I had far grander things planned for us."

Had. Past tense. She braced herself for a confrontation. It had been a long time coming. "I do, Hunter. It's all I ever wanted. When did you start planning something different? Because I seem to recall, you promised we would settle down and have a normal life together."

Hunter made a sound of disgust and slashed at the air with his hand. "Do you really think I could settle down after all the things I've done? Think again, sister. I'm facing a life on the road."

"On the run, you mean." She'd not felt this bleak since the day they'd fled their guardian's house more than three years ago.

"I did it all for you," he reminded testily.

"I am grateful to you for extricating me from our uncle. I owe you my life, Hunter."

"But," he ground out.

"But I never agreed to the path you chose for us. I've never been at peace with it. I've done nothing but pray for God's forgiveness every night for my part in it."

"Huh? What part?" He snorted. "I've gone out of my way to keep your lily-white hands clean."

"Again, I thank you," she sighed, "but we can't go on like this," she repeated, "I have to choose my own path now."

He rounded on her in fury. "You make it sound like I had a choice."

"Everyone has a choice," she noted sadly. Not always a good choice, but a choice nonetheless.

"You were barely alive," he spat, stalking closer. "At death's door. I had to do something to pay your doctor bills."

"Please don't, Hunter." She blinked back tears. "I cannot bear to fight with you."

"You want an apology, eh? You want me to confess my sins? Perhaps turn myself in to the law?" He fingered the pistol in his holster. "Well, I cannot, Jane. I cannot, because it wouldn't be honest. The truth is, I would do everything I did all over again to keep you alive and safe, to keep you here with me this side of glory," he snarled. "You deserved to live. To grow up. To be happy."

He was referring to the last night of abuse at their uncle's house, the night that had broken something inside him. Jane's heart wept to hear the suffering in his voice after all these years. "I *am* happy, Hunter. Happier than I've ever been, don't you see?" She spread her arms and did a little twirl for him in her red dress. "Because of you, I am alive and well, and now I wish to settle in Headstone. I wish to make a new life for myself here."

"You mean for us to part ways, then?"

"You know I never wanted that." Her voice trembled. "I would have preferred to settle down together as we always planned, but you've stated that is impossible. I met someone special, someone I plan to marry. That is why I wish to stay here."

"One of those cocky Barra brothers." Hunter's voice turned sly and surly. "I've met him."

"When?" Jane's blood chilled. "Where is he?" she demanded, as the cool finality in Hunter's voice sank in. "What have you done with him?" Dodge had stepped outside to search for his father. "Please assure me he is still alive."

Hunter gave a mirthless laugh. "See for yourself, dear sister." He lit a lantern and held it up to illuminate the small chamber.

Dodge was sitting in a chair in the center of the room, his head bowed and his arms hanging limply at his sides. Jane gave a choking cry and flew to him. She slid to her knees before him. "Oh, my darling! Are you alright? Speak to me," she pleaded through numb lips.

To her surprise, the edges of his mouth quirked slightly upward at her pleading. Then he moved so quickly, she had no time to catch her breath. One moment he was sitting like a limp rag doll; and the next moment she was standing behind him.

"Don't fight my brother, Dodge," she pleaded. "I'm begging you. Don't let it come to that." Her voice broke. "I love you both so much." If it came to a gunfight, one of them would be lying dead when it was over.

"I know, chickabiddy." Dodge's voice was gentle but firm. "That's why your brother has a decision to make. Either give me your blessing, Sherrington, or shoot me now; because I'm never going to stop loving your sister."

Hunter stalked the room in front of them, hands never far from his weapons.

"Sure and you can take our Jane back on the road," Dodge wheedled, "but you'll spend the rest of your days protecting her from the likes of unsavory men, from stray bullets, and from the next arrest. Give me your blessing, and I'll keep her far away from all those things. I'll love her, cherish her, and protect her with my life until I cock up my toes."

A shot sounded in the distance. Though it was still raining outside, the thunder had abated enough for them to hear it.

Hunter stiffened and grew still as if listening, confirming Jane's suspicions that the shots they'd heard earlier were a signal of some sort. Another three shots were fired in quick succession, just like before.

Hunter turned back to Jane. "We are out of time. Are you coming with me?" There was a world of heartache in his eyes, as if he already knew her answer.

She pressed closer to Dodge. "If you truly love me, you will let me go, Hunter. You will leave me behind this time."

His upper lip curled in a snarl. "I truly love you, sister. I always have and always will." He backed towards the door. At the last minute, he whipped out a pistol and aimed it at Dodge. "You'd best pray every day that you make her happy, Barra. Otherwise, I'll come back and put you in the ground." With that, he disappeared into the gloomy outdoors.

"I will," Dodge promised to the closed door.

Jane ran to the window to peer after her brother, but he was gone. The storm was picking up again, rain sheeting down so hard and so quickly that it made no sense to step back out in it just yet. "Dodge!" she whirled around to find him standing directly behind her. "Oh, Dodge!" She threw her arms around his neck but gentled her embrace when he winced. "You're hurt!" she cried in horror, drawing back.

"I'm fine," he assured, cuddling her closer.

"Is your nose broken?" She reached up to lightly probe the appendage with her fingertips.

"I don't believe so."

"What happened? Why did you come to blows with my brother?"

"We didn't come to blows, chickabiddy. I merely asked him for your hand in marriage. We discussed it like men, and he saw the light."

"Discussed it like men, eh?" Jane spat, caressing his bruised face. "I've a good mind to—"

"Kiss me, Jane." He brushed his swollen and cracked lips against her jawline.

With a soft sigh of surrender, she touched her mouth to his. It was a long time before they spoke again.

Afterwards, Jane laid her head against Dodge's shoulder, while he idly stroked a hand through her hair.

"I had to face him, chickabiddy. It was the only way. Otherwise, he'd have just kept coming back for you."

"I know." She cuddled closer, thankful they'd lived to tell the tale.

"He was only testing me. He wasn't trying to hurt me. Not really. He had to make sure I was up to the task of taking care of the only person in the world he cares for."

"Will you go after him?" Jane was almost afraid to ask, not wanting to contemplate him being put in a position that would stretch his loyalties to the limit.

"I'm neither a sheriff nor a marshal. Bringing your brother to justice is not my job. Making his sister happy, however, is." Dodge nuzzled the soft skin at her temple. Then he drew back to take a knee before her. "Will you marry me, Jinglebell Jane?"

She caught her breath. Dodge had a way of doing things and acting so quickly sometimes that it made her head spin. "Yes, you loco cowboy." She tugged at his hands, trying to get him to stand.

He rose and towered over her with a look so tender it took her breath away. "You'll catch up on your schooling first. There's no need for us to rush into anything."

"What? Are you getting cold feet already?" she teased. It

would probably be best for Dodge to put a ring on her finger soon, in the event her brother came back to check on them.

"Then again," he swooped in for a kiss that stole the air from her lungs, "if we decide we can't wait a day longer to be together as man and wife, at least you'll have a live-in tutor."

"I like the sound of that," she sighed. "As soon as this rain lets up, we should go celebrate."

"How do you want to celebrate, chickabiddy? Your wish is my command."

She nearly melted at the affection in his eyes. "I want to go with you to the town square and see the Christmas tree." The one Sheriff Otera said there'd been a special lighting ceremony for. This was her town now, so it was her tree, too.

"Consider it done, my lady. I reckon I had you pegged right when I called you my Jinglebell Jane." All the hope and joy of the season was in his voice.

EPILOGUE

DODGE

*B*efore the day was through, a hue and a cry rose in Headstone at the discovery that all the members of Hunter Sherrington's gang had escaped from jail. Not only had they escaped, three banks in the surrounding areas had been robbed about the same time. It made no sense. Every man in custody had been kept under lock and key. Their meals had been carefully rationed out, their spare clothing and bedrolls searched multiple times per day for weapons, and they'd not been allowed visitors. Well, their visits had been severely limited.

Only a few individuals had access — the sheriff and his deputies, the federal marshals, Felicity in the capacity of an attorney who'd stood by to represent Jane if needed, and another attorney who'd traveled in from Tombstone to represent the rest of the accused. All efforts to contact the second attorney had proven to be in vain, so far. It was likely he'd been part of the escape plan.

To Dodge's dismay, Jane was called into the sheriff's office the next morning for another long round of questioning. He paced the street outside, fuming over the indignities she was having to endure when she should have been in school. Jane was a Barra now, or rather, she would be soon when they said their vows. He couldn't fathom how their kindhearted sheriff could possibly hold Jane responsible for the escape of her brother's gang.

Stuffing his hands deep in his pocket, Dodge mulled over the strange set of gunshots. They'd happened both earlier and later in the day yesterday. What was their significance? Jane had been so certain they were a signal, but what did the shots mean and how had they helped Sherrington and his men skip town so swiftly? Like bloody ghosts! Here one second and gone the next.

A commotion in the street had his head spinning. A gold-gilded carriage, bearing a family crest, careened in his direction and skidded to a muddy halt in front of the sheriff's office. None other than Colt Branson hopped down. His Stetson and suit were askew, his longish brown hair flying in all directions. A couple launched themselves from the carriage in his wake. Dodge recognized them as Colt's brother, Jordan, and his new wife, Olivia. Both were from the east and were expected to return there soon. Dodge was surprised they were still in town.

"Where is she?" Colt demanded, stalking in Dodge's direction.

Dodge raised a brow at him. "Who?"

"That blasted sister of Sherrington's, that's who!"

Is that so? Dodge stepped nose-to-nose with the man, feeling a stab of unholy delight to discover he towered a good inch or two over him. "Just so we're clear, Jane is my affianced now. I'll thank you to tread carefully with whatever you have to say next."

"He took her!" Colt spluttered. "Hunter Sherrington took my sister!"

"MaryAnne is gone?" Dodge stared in astonishment and growing alarm at the two brothers and Olivia.

"Goner than gone," Colt retorted icily. "We'd just gotten her back, too." He pushed past Dodge, crossed the porch of the jailhouse, and threw open the door despite the protests of the guard standing there.

Dodge jogged after him.

"Sir! Sir, please!" Sheriff Otera shot to his feet from behind his desk where he'd been questioning Jane.

To Dodge's relief, Jane looked calm and at ease.

When Colt moved in her direction with determination, however, alarm settled over her features. The sheriff quickly stepped between them. "This is a private interview, Mr. Branson. You know the rules."

"My sister is missing!" Colt seethed over the sheriff's shoulder at Jane. "I don't reckon you have anything to say about that?"

Dodge took the opportunity to rush to the side of his beloved. He slung an arm around her shoulders. "You don't have to answer that, chickabiddy."

"But I will." Jane's voice shook. "MaryAnne's betrayal of my brother never made sense until now, I'm afraid."

"Betrayal!" Colt was fast losing his wits. He resembled a rabid wolf foaming at the mouth. "MaryAnne was working with the federal marshals. She was on the right side of the law."

"Was she?" Jane inquired softly. She held up her hands when Colt resumed his blustering. "I am not saying your sister doesn't have a good heart. She did me many good turns while we were on the road, but she did more than that — far more. She fell in love."

"What?" Jordan leaped into action and joined his brother's side. "How can you say such a thing? She was being held captive by your brother."

Jane shook her head mutely.

"I rather think she has the right of it," Olivia cut in softly, gliding forward to take her husband's hand. "You remember what I said the day you rescued me from their gang, Jordan? MaryAnne seemed to be in charge."

"She was working undercover," Jordan protested. "She already explained all that to us."

"Maybe," Jane was no longer certain about MaryAnne's loyalties, "and maybe not."

"Explain!" Colt roared, eyes spitting so much fire at Jane that Dodge shoved her partly behind him.

"I wasn't supposed to ever speak of it," she quavered. "They swore me to secrecy for MaryAnne's safety, but I reckon it's time for me to break my silence at long last." She sighed, and Dodge tensed.

Do not say too much, my little chickabiddy. "Maybe you should wait for Felicity to get here," he muttered in her ear.

"I've done nothing wrong," she assured at a whisper. "Let me say my piece."

After a long, searching look, he nodded.

"MaryAnne was betrothed to a banker in the next town over. He wrote for a mail-order bride; but when she arrived to town, he acted more interested in bedding her than marrying her. From what I understand, an opportunity arose for him to make a match of it with a more prominent family. It wasn't a love match, mind you, but he couldn't resist the dowry. At any rate, it left MaryAnne severely compromised. When she tried to leave town, however, the banker locked her in his vault, where she was discovered during a heist, barely alive, by Hunter and his posse of robbers."

Colt shuddered and scrubbed a shaking hand down his face. "Go on."

Jane shook her head, wishing what she had to share was any easier. "Hunter canceled the heist and turned it into a rescue operation, instead. I never saw him make over another person like that. He personally nursed MaryAnne back to health. By the time she was recovered, she'd become the second person in the world Hunter cared about — second only to me, or so I thought." She gave them a sad smile. "Somewhere along the way, she passed me up and became his number one. His confidante. His right hand. He included her in his life in ways he'd never included me." It was a position Jane had almost envied at the time. Almost.

Jordan groaned and half turned away. "I don't think I can take much more of this." Olivia was there to gather him in her arms and offer comfort.

Colt had visibly deflated. "Are you saying my sister has become a criminal?" He looked shattered and lost. "All three of those banks that were robbed yesterday belonged to the same man."

Dodge stared as the realization dawned on them all. Maybe the bank heists had been more than regular heists. What if they were part of a carefully planned revenge? Now that was something to mull on!

Jane shot Colt a sympathetic look, clearly loathing the thought of wounding him further. "All I am saying is she is a woman in love.

"With your brother?"

"I believe so, yes."

"I still don't understand something." Olivia frowned. "That day on Rose de la Montaña, I saw MaryAnne shoot a squirrel. She was with another man who shot down two more squirrels and kissed her afterwards. If she was so in love with your brother, why would she …oh!" she sighed. "It was him all this time, wasn't it?"

Jane nodded. "It was him."

"Then how did he escape capture if he was on the mountain with the others when the federal marshals arrived?" Olivia cried.

Jane shook her head, signifying to Dodge she truly didn't know.

He had his own suspicions now that Jane had cast Mary-Anne in a different light. Poor Colt and Jordan Branson! He couldn't imagine what they were going through at the moment. They'd built their entire mail-order bride business on the hope of helping would-be brides like their sister who'd disappeared shortly after she headed west. Their Gallant Rescuer Insurance clause additionally put them in the business of rescuing damsels in distress. It was a conundrum for sure and one only they could figure out in time.

Jordan cast a harried look in Sheriff Otera's direction. "You'll still look for her, won't you?"

The sheriff nodded, not quite meeting Jordan's gaze.

"Because I never intend to stop. She's not well." Jordan's voice dropped to a pleading note as he hugged his wife. "She needs help."

The expressions of those gathered said otherwise. Dodge glanced down at Jane, but she gave a slight shake of her head as if begging him to say no more.

"Are you ready to head back to the ranch, chickabiddy?" he inquired softly.

She nodded, a faint smile warming her pale features.

"In that case," he raised his voice and boomed, "unless you're charging my future bride with something, sheriff..."

"No. No charges." Sheriff Otera waved them on with a grim expression. He had bigger problems to attend to now that Jane had given her statement. He motioned to the Bransons. "If you'll just take a seat, all three of you."

Dodge guided Jane outside to the street where his horse was waiting. He could've borrowed a wagon from Levi, but he hadn't bothered. Jane was all bundled up in a riding habit and coat, and they both preferred the outdoors — and how close sharing a horse allowed them to sit in plain view of the public.

She snuggled against his sore chest and mid-section the moment she was mounted up. He hadn't yet told her about how many punches he'd taken to the gut and truly didn't mind the pain. It was a small cost to pay for securing her brother's blessing and a happy reminder that he and Jane would be wed soon.

"As soon as we get back to the ranch, I have a salve to apply to that split lip of yours." She fussed over him, smoothing his lapels.

He waited until they were clear of Main Street and all their witnesses before hooking an arm around her waist and tugging her closer. "About that salve, do you have it on you?"

"I do." She reached inside her reticule and came up with a small tube. "Why? Is your lip bothering you right now?"

"Something awful," he lied, slowing his horse to a walk.

Looking concerned, she hastily removed a glove and reached up to apply a drop of it on his lips. The moment she started to rub it in, he started to kiss her fingers. She chuckled and rolled her eyes knowingly at him. "All better now?"

"Not quite. I think you need to rub it in a little more. Like this." Before she could respond, he dipped his head closer and claimed her mouth in a thorough kiss.

"Dodge Barra," she sighed when he raised his head. "You're something else, but I love you for it. So very much."

"I can live with that." He grinned down at her. "I love you, too, Jinglebell Jane, with all my heart and strength. And I'm going to spend the rest of my days proving it to you." *And your brother.* Dodge reckoned they hadn't seen the last of Hunter Sherrington. It was best to be ready when he turned up again.

Thank you for reading
JINGLEBELL JANE!
Keep turning the page for a sneak peek at
Mail Order Brides Rescue Series #8
Absentminded Amelia.

An absentminded school teacher, a cowboy rancher with a spirited niece and nephew in his custody, and a marriage of convenience to solve all of their problems — or create new ones!

SNEAK PREVIEW:
ABSENTMINDED AMELIA

*A*melia Cornwall stumbled in shock to her dormitory room at the Boston Park Orphanage, barely making it to her cot before she burst into tears. She'd just been dismissed from her duties as a music instructor by the headmistress.

The room was so cold that her tears felt like sleet sliding icily down her cheeks. According to the headmistress, the orphanage was flat broke, so the board was being forced to economize in every way possible. All through the month of November, Amelia had suffered the cold, the lack of candles to spare, and the sparse food rations all the instructors had been placed on. However, she did not understand — not for a second — the need to turn her out into the streets with nothing more than a simple thank you for her last three years of service. There wasn't even enough money left in the school coffers to pay her final wages.

Mercy! What am I going to do? Amelia could hardly produce a coherent thought, much less form a plan. She was too numb on the inside. *I am doomed, utterly doomed, that's what!*

She had no family, no place to go, and a desperately small savings in which to support herself until she figured out what came next.

She reached blindly for her threadbare cloak and hood hanging from a hook behind her cot. *Where, oh where, is my travel bag?* She seemed to recall lending it out to a co-worker last Christmas, but — for the life of her — she couldn't recall receiving it back. It hadn't seemed important at the time, because she possessed no family or friends with which to spend the holidays, and she'd never really pictured herself leaving the orphanage. And now she wasn't being given a choice...

Drawing a shuddery breath that turned into a silent sob, Amelia drew her spare navy wool gown from the other hook and rolled her few belongings inside it — a set of embroidered pillow cases she'd pieced together from flour sacks, a tarnished silver brush the school officials claimed once belonged to a family relation of hers, and an iron key that had been in her pocket the day she'd been turned over to the orphanage. She was three-years-old at the time. She had no memory of her life before the orphanage and was terrified at the thought of trying to eke out any sort of existence outside its gray stone walls at the age of one and twenty.

Amelia's boot slid on something papery as she turned to face the doorway that would lead to the enormous lonely world beyond it. She drearily bent to pick up the scrap of paper and noted it was a discarded newspaper clipping, an old one from the yellowed look of it. The headline of an advert caught her eye:

Boomtown Mail Order Brides: The only mail order bride company with an insurance policy enforced by the Gallant Rescue Society — No extra cost!

She gave a horrified squeak at the thought of some bright

and promising young woman of a marriageable age, being ordered up by a stranger through the mail. *Sweet heavens!* If she was reading the advert correctly, the prospective bride would be expected to hop on a train in short order, travel west, and marry the hopeful groom sight unseen.

She shivered. Only a truly desperate woman would ever consider doing something so outlandishly brazen, so deplorably scandalous!

A truly desperate creature. Her thoughts came to a complete and sudden stand-still. *Like me!*

I hope you enjoyed this excerpt from
Absentminded Amelia.

This complete 12-book series is available now in eBook, paperback, and Kindle Unlimited on Amazon.

Read them all!
Hot-Tempered Hannah
Cold-Feet Callie
Fiery Felicity
Misunderstood Meg
Dare-Devil Daisy
Outrageous Olivia
Jinglebell Jane
Absentminded Amelia
Bookish Belinda
Tenacious Trudy
Meddlesome Madge
Mismatched MaryAnne
MOB Rescue Series Box Set Books 1-4

MOB Rescue Series Box Set Books 5-8
MOB Rescue Series Box Set Books 9-12

Much love,
Jovie

GET A FREE BOOK!

Join my mailing list to be the first to know about new releases, free books, special discount prices, Bonus Content, and giveaways.

https://BookHip.com/GNVABPD

NOTE FROM JOVIE

Guess what? I have some Bonus Content for you. Read a little more about the swoony cowboy heroes in my books by signing up for my mailing list.

There will be a special Bonus Content chapter for each new

book I write, just for my subscribers. Plus, you get a FREE book just for signing up!

Thank you for reading and loving my books.

JOIN CUPPA JO READERS!

If you're on Facebook, you're invited to join my group, Cuppa Jo Readers. Saddle up for some fun reader games and giveaways + book chats about my sweet and swoon-worthy cowboy book heroes!

https://www.facebook.com/groups/CuppaJoReaders

SNEAK PEEK: BRIDE FOR THE INNKEEPER

January, 1892 — Albuquerque, New Mexico

*L*acey Cleveland pulled up the hood of her cloak. She remained in the shadows of the alley between two clapboard buildings as she adjusted the precious bundle against her shoulder. Her tiny nephew was fast asleep beneath a faded patchwork quilt, the last memento she had of her late sister who'd been a magician with a needle and thread. For the thousandth time, she experienced an enormous sense of gratitude that the toddler was still so young. By the grace of God, the eleven-month-old would remain oblivious to the many troubles they were facing, the least of which was their desperate need to flee from New Mexico.

I will keep us safe from him, little one, if it's the last thing I do. With one last furtive glance down the alley to ensure they weren't being followed, she finally stepped into the full blast of morning sunlight. It was early, barely eight o'clock. She planned on being the first customer to darken the door of the mail-order bride agency in Albuquerque.

Though her knees trembled with apprehension, she walked without looking to the right or the left. It was an old trick her gypsy parents had taught her. *May they rest in peace.* When a person held their head high and moved with purpose, they were less likely to be questioned. Or beheld with suspicion. Or even noticed, for that matter.

Out of the corner of her eye, she watched a farmer rattle past on the cobblestone street with his wagon full of milk jugs. Though he tipped his hat in her general direction, she could tell he was paying her no real mind.

Another block of walking brought her to her destination. She slowed her steps at the sight of the cheerful sign, freshly painted white letters on a dark blue background. *Albuquerque Mail-Order Bride Agency.* Good gracious, but her life had sunk to a new low at the necessity of darkening the door of such an outlandish establishment! *Forgive me, Lord, for what I am about to do.* Answering the advert felt all too much like selling herself on an auction block, but she was fresh out of better ideas. If marrying a perfect stranger was what it took to get her and her nephew safely out of town, then she was willing.

"May I help you, ma'am?" A matronly looking woman, wearing a somber high-neck gown of green wool, was seated behind an antique cherry wood desk. She glanced over the tops of her spectacles, eyeing Lacey from her simple up-do to her dusty boots.

"Yes, please." The thready sound of Lacey's voice wasn't the least bit contrived. She felt close to fainting as she breathlessly rattled off her carefully rehearsed speech. "My family suffered a terrible tragedy, which left me alone in the world with no money and a little one to raise on my own. I can see no other recourse but to marry with haste." It was the closest explanation she could give to the truth without outright lying.

To her relief, the woman's severe expression relaxed at

the mention of the babe in her arms. Her thin lips wavered into a faint smile as she rose. "Have a seat, please." She waved one angular hand at the cozy overstuffed chair parked in front of her desk. "I'll fetch some refreshments."

Over the course of the next hour, Lacey was fed, counseled on the merits of signing a mail-order bride contract, and successfully bound by her signature to marry a man by the name of Edward Remington.

"He's an innkeeper in a town bearing the lovely name of Christmas Mountain," the woman sighed. "Doesn't it sound like something straight from a storybook?"

It did, but life had taught Lacey that looks and sounds could be frightfully deceiving. The fact remained, she was about to become wed to a man she'd never met, a man she could only hope would treat her and her nephew better than her jailbird of a brother-in-law.

"Are you certain he will not balk at the notion of me arriving with a babe in my arms?" Her thoughts swam dizzily as she pondered the possibility that Mr. Remington might have no interest in becoming a father, at least not so soon.

The matchmaker shrugged. "He did not rule out the possibility of marrying a widow, though our application most certainly gave him the option."

Lacey caught her breath, wondering if she should set the woman straight on her marital status. She'd not been previously wed, much less widowed. After an inner debate, however, she decided it was wiser to let the woman assume her husband was deceased. Disclosing that her brother-in-law was behind bars might increase the chances of her whereabouts being reported back to him.

"How soon may I wed this Mr. Remington?" she inquired nervously.

"I can have you on the mid-morning train, if you wish." The woman smiled in understanding. "Mr. Remington has provided a generous allowance for your travels. Enough, I dare say, to provide for the sustenance of both you and your babe."

Lacey momentarily closed her eyes against the sting of grateful tears. "How can I ever thank you?" she whispered.

"By becoming the best innkeeper's wife in the west," the woman retorted, leaning forward in her chair to sort through the required paperwork. "Arranging another successful marriage will bolster our company's reputation, as well as our profits."

The best innkeeper's wife in the west? Oh, my! It was a tall order, indeed. A wry chuckle chased away Lacey's tears. Until now, she'd been so focused on survival that she'd not given a single thought about whether her groom would find her suitable for *his* needs.

Good gracious! If she was being perfectly honest with herself, she didn't know the first thing about running an inn. A wave of uncertainty swept over her as she pondered the many things she would undoubtedly have to learn. Even so, a clean, well-run inn sounded like the perfect place to raise a child. He would have a roof over his head and plenty of food in his belly.

Shaking off the tendrils of self-doubt, Lacey lifted her chin and met the matchmaker's gaze. "I would be delighted to catch that mid-morning train."

I hope you enjoyed this excerpt from
Bride for the Innkeeper.
Available now on in eBook, paperback, and Kindle Unlimited on Amazon.

Read the whole trilogy!

Bride for the Innkeeper
Bride for the Deputy
Bride for the Tribal Chief

Much love,
Jovie

SNEAK PEEK: ELIZABETH

Early November, 1866

*E*lizabeth Byrd rubbed icy hands up and down her arms beneath her threadbare navy wool cloak as she gingerly hopped down from the stagecoach. It was so much colder in northern Texas than it had been in Georgia. She gazed around her at the hard-packed earthen streets, scored by the ruts of many wagon wheels. They probably would have been soft and muddy if it weren't for the brisk winds swirling above them. Instead, they were stiff with cold and covered in a layer of frost that glinted like rosy crystals beneath the setting sun.

Plain, saltbox buildings of weathered gray planks hovered over the streets like watchful sentinels, as faded and tattered as the handful of citizens scurrying past — women in faded gingham dresses and bonnets along with a half-dozen or so men in work clothes and dusty top hats. More than likely, they were in a hurry to get home, since it was fast approaching the dinner hour. Her stomach rumbled out a contentious reminder at how long it had been since her own last meal.

So this was Cowboy Creek.

At least I'll fit in. She glanced ruefully down at her workaday brown dress and the scuffed toes of her boots. Perhaps, wearing the castoffs of her former maid, Lucy, wasn't the most brilliant idea she'd ever come up with. However, it was the only plan she'd been able to conjure up on such short notice. A young woman traveling alone couldn't be too careful these days. For her own safety, she'd wanted to attract as little attention as possible during her long journey west. It had worked. Few folks had given her more than a cursory glance the entire trip, leaving her plenty of time to silently berate herself for accepting the challenge of her dear friend, Caroline, to change her stars by becoming a mail-order bride like she and a few other friends had done the previous Christmas.

"Thanks to the war, there's nothing left for us here in Atlanta, love. You know it, and I know it," Caroline had chided gently. Then she'd leaned in to embrace her tenderly. "I know you miss him. We all do." She was referring to Elizabeth's fiancé who'd perished in battle. "But he would want you to go on and keep living. That means dusting off your broken heart and finding a man to marry while you're still young enough to have a family of your own."

She and her friends were in their early twenties, practically rusticating on the shelf in the eyes of those who'd once comprised the social elite in Atlanta. They were confirmed spinsters, yesterday's news, has-beens…

Well, only Elizabeth was now. Her friends had proven to be more adventurous than she was. They'd responded to the advert a year earlier, journeyed nearly all the way across the continent, and were now happily married.

Or so they claimed. Elizabeth was still skeptical about the

notion of agreeing to marry a man she'd never met. However, Caroline's latest letter had been full of nothing but praise about the successful matches she and their friends had made.

Be assured, dearest, that there are still scads of marriageable men lined up and waiting for you in Cowboy Creek. All you have to do is pack your bags and hop on a train. We cannot wait to see you again!

Caroline had been the one to discover this startling opportunity by reading an advert in The Western Gentlemen's Gazette. It had been placed there by a businessman who claimed to be running the fastest growing mail-order bride company in the west.

All I had to do is pack my bags and leave behind everyone and everything I've ever known to take part in the same opportunity. Elizabeth shivered and pulled her cloak more tightly around her. Attempting to duck her chin farther down inside the collar, she wondered if she'd just made the biggest mistake of her life. She was in Cowboy Creek several days later than she'd originally agreed to arrive, having wrestled like the dickens with her better judgment to make up her mind to join her friends.

Oh, how she missed the three of them! Caroline, Daphne, and Violet were former debutantes from Atlanta, like herself. All were from impoverished families whose properties and bank accounts had been devastated by the war. It was the only reason Elizabeth had been willing to even consider the foolish idea of joining them. She was fast running out of options. Her widowed mother was barely keeping food on the table for her three younger sisters.

Even so, it had been a last-minute decision, one she'd made too late to begin any correspondence with her intended groom. She didn't even know the man's name, only that he would be waiting for her in Cowboy Creek when her stagecoach rolled into town. Or so Caroline had promised.

With a sigh of resignation, Elizabeth reached down to grasp the handles of her two travel bags that the stage driver had unloaded for her. The rest of her belongings would arrive in the coming days. There'd been too many trunks to bring along by stage. In the meantime, she hoped and prayed she was doing the right thing for her loved ones. At worst, her reluctant decision to leave home meant one less mouth for Mama to feed. At best, she might claw her way back to some modicum of social significance and be in the position to help her family in some way. Some day…

Her hopes in that regard plummeted the second she laid eyes on the two men in the wagon rumbling in her direction. It was a rickety vehicle with no overhead covering. It creaked and groaned with each turn of its wheels, a problem that might have easily been solved with a squirt of oil. Then again, the heavily patched trousers of both men indicated they were as poor as church mice. More than likely, they didn't possess any extra coin for oil.

Of all the rotten luck! She bit her lower lip. *I'm about to marry a man as poor as myself.* So much for her hopes of improving her lot in life enough to send money home to Mama and the girls!

The driver slowed his team, a pair of red-brown geldings. They were much lovelier than the rattle-trap they were pulling. "Elizabeth Byrd, I presume?" he inquired in a rich baritone that was neither unpleasant nor overly warm and welcoming.

Her insides froze to a block of ice. This time, it wasn't because of the frigid temperatures of northern Texas. She recognized that face, that voice; and with them, came a flood of heart wrenching emotions.

"You!" she exclaimed. Her travel bags slid from her nerveless fingers to the ground once more. A hand flew to her heart, as she relived the sickening dread all over again that she'd experienced at the Battle of James Island. She was the unlucky nurse who'd delivered the message to Captain David Pemberton that his wife had passed during childbirth. The babe hadn't survived, either. But what, in heaven's name, was the tragic officer doing so far from home? Unless she was mistaken, his family was from the Ft. Sumpter area.

"Nurse Byrd." The captain handed his reins to the man sitting next to him, a grizzled older fellow who was dressed in a well-pressed brown suit, though both knees bore patches. "We meet again." He offered her a two-fingered salute and reached for her travel bags. He was even more handsome than she remembered, despite the well-worn Stetson shading his piercing bourbon eyes. During their last encounter, he'd been clean shaven. His light brown sideburns now traveled down to a shortly clipped beard. If the offbeat rhythm of her heart was any indication, he wore the more rugged look rather nicely.

Which was neither here nor there. Elizabeth gave herself a mental shake. She'd been searching for a sign, anything that would shed light on whether she was doing the right thing by coming to Cowboy Creek. Encountering this man, of all people, only a handful of minutes after her arrival, seemed a pretty clear indication of just how horrible a mistake she'd made.

She nudged the handles of her bags with the toe of her boot to put them out of reach. "Y-you don't have to go through with this, captain. I can only imagine how difficult it is for you to lay eyes on me again." If it was anything close to how difficult it was for her to lay eyes on him, it would behoove them both to take off running in opposite directions. "I am quite happy to board with one of my friends until I can secure passage back to Georgia." The whole trip had been a horrible miscalculation of judgment. She could see that now as she stared stonily into the face of the officer who'd led the man to whom she was once affianced into the battle that had claimed his life. Captain Pemberton didn't know that wretched fact, of course. How could he? They were neither personally, nor closely, acquainted at the time.

The expression in his eyes softened a few degrees as he regarded her. "I gather you found the young man you were searching for during the war?" he noted quietly. "Otherwise, you would not be here."

Preparing to marry you, you mean! "I found him, yes." Her voice was tight with cold and misery. It was all she could do to keep her teeth from chattering. "I found him and buried him."

"Ah." He nodded sadly. "Words are never adequate in situations like these. Nevertheless, I am deeply sorry for your loss."

His regret appeared genuine. She sensed he was a kind man, a good man, despite the deplorable circumstances under which they'd made their first acquaintance. *More's the pity!* Though she couldn't exactly hold the captain responsible for the Union bullet that had taken her Charley's life, she couldn't just up and marry the man responsible for leading him into harm's way, either. Could she?

Perhaps it was the cold breeze numbing her brain, but suddenly she was no longer certain about a good number of things.

"Come, Elizabeth." The commanding note in David Pemberton's voice brooked no further arguments. "You must be famished after such a long journey, and you'll catch your death out here if we linger in the cold."

This time, Elizabeth's toes were too icy to function when he reached for her travel bags. She stood there shivering while he tossed them inside his wagon. She was both shocked and grateful when he proceeded to unbutton his overcoat and slide it around her shoulders.

It was toasty warm from his body heat and smelled woodsy and masculine. "I th-thank y-you." She was no longer able to hide how badly her teeth were chattering.

"Think nothing of it, Miss Byrd." He slid a protective arm around her shoulders and guided her on down the street. "A friendly fellow named Frederick owns the eatery next door. Since our wedding isn't for another two hours, how about we head over there for a spell? We can grab a bite to eat and thaw out at the same time."

Our wedding? Her lips parted in protest, but she was shivering too hard to form any words.

As if sensing her confusion, he smiled and leaned closer to speak directly in her ear. His breath warmed her chilly lobe and sent a shot of...something straight down to her toes. "Surely an angel of mercy like yourself can spare the time to swap a few war stories with an old soldier?"

She clamped her teeth together. *An angel of mercy, indeed!* She'd felt more like an angel of death back there on the battlefield. There were days she lost more soldiers than the ones she managed to save. It was something she preferred never to think of again, much less discuss.

"If I cannot make you smile at least once in the next two hours, I'll purchase your passage back to Atlanta, myself," he teased, tightening his arm around her shoulders.

Now *that* was an offer she couldn't afford to pass up. She didn't currently possess the coin for a return trip, though she had to wonder if the shabbily dressed captain was any better for the funds, himself.

She gave him a tight-lipped nod and allowed him to lead her inside the eatery.

The tantalizing aromas of fresh-baked bread, hot cider,

and some other delectable entrée assailed them, making her mouth water. A pine tree graced one corner of the dining area. Its boughs were weighed down with festive gingerbread ornaments and countless strands of red ribbon. A man in a white apron, whom she could only presume was Captain Pemberton's friend, Frederick, cut between a line of tables and hurried in their direction, arms outstretched. "You rebel you! Someone might have at least warned me you were one of the lucky fellers gittin' himself a new wife."

"Oh-h!" Elizabeth's voice came out as a warble of alarm as, from the corner of her eye, she watched a young serving woman heading their way from the opposite direction. She was bearing a tray with a tall cake and holding it in such a manner that she couldn't see over the top of it. She was very much at risk of running in to someone or something.

David Pemberton glanced down at her concern, but all she could do was wave her hand in the direction of the calamity about to take place.

His gaze swiftly followed where she pointed, just in time to watch the unfortunate server and her cake collide with Frederick. White icing and peach preserves flew everywhere. His hair and one side of his face were plastered with a layer of sticky whiteness.

The woman gave a strangled shriek and slid to her knees. A puppy dashed out of nowhere and began to lick the remains of the gooey fluff from her fingers.

Afterwards, Elizabeth would blame it on the long journey for frazzling her nerves to such an extent; because, otherwise, there was no excuse on heaven or earth for what she did next.

She laughed — hysterically! It was ill-mannered of her, unladylike to the extreme, and completely uncalled for, but she couldn't help it. She laughed until there were tears in her eyes.

Captain Pemberton grinned in unholy glee at her. There was such a delicious glint in his whiskey eyes that it made her knees tremble.

"A deal's a deal, nurse; and the way I see it, you did more than smile. You laughed, which means I'll not be needing to purchase that trip back to Atlanta for you, after all. Unless you've any further objections, we've a little less than two hours before we say our vows." He arched one dark brow at her in challenge.

Their gazes clashed, and the world beneath her shifted. As a woman of her word, she suddenly couldn't come up with any more reasons — not a blessed one — why they couldn't or shouldn't get married.

Tonight!

I hope you enjoyed this excerpt from
Elizabeth
Available now on in eBook, paperback, and Kindle Unlimited on Amazon.

Read the whole trilogy!
Elizabeth
Grace
Lilly

Much love,
Jovie

ALSO BY JOVIE

For the most up-to-date printable list of my sweet historical books:

Click here

or go to:

https://www.jografford.com/joviegracebooks

For the most up-to-date printable list of my sweet contemporary books:

Click here

or go to:

https://www.JoGrafford.com/books

ABOUT JOVIE

Jovie Grace is an Amazon bestselling author of sweet and inspirational historical romance books full of faith, family, and second chances. She also writes sweet contemporary romance as Jo Grafford.

1.) Follow on Amazon!
https://www.amazon.com/stores/Jovie-Grace/author/
B09SB1V58Q

2.) Join Cuppa Jo Readers!
https://www.facebook.com/groups/CuppaJoReaders

3.) Follow on Bookbub!
https://www.bookbub.com/authors/jovie-grace

4.) Follow on Facebook!
https://www.facebook.com/JovieGraceBooks

amazon.com/stores/Jovie-Grace/author/B09SB1V58Q

bookbub.com/authors/jovie-grace

facebook.com/JovieGraceBooks

Made in the USA
Middletown, DE
22 August 2024